McGowan's Return

Also by Rob Smith:

McGowan's Call (fiction)
McGowan's Retreat (fiction)
Night Voices (fiction)
Hogwarts, Narnia, and Middle Earth (criticism)
256 Zones of Gray (poetry)

McGowan's Return

Rob Smith

This book is a work of fiction. As such, names, characters, incidents, and places (real or imagined) are used fictitiously and are products of the author's imagination. Any resemblance to persons or actual events is coincidental.

Cover design and photograph by Drinian Press

Drinian Press, LLC
P.O. Box 63
Huron, Ohio 44839
Visit our Web site at: www.DrinianPress.com

Library of Congress Control Number: 2011922593

ISBN-10: 0-9833069-0-7
ISBN-13: 978-0-9833069-0-0

Printed in the United States of America

Greater Cleveland

Chapter 1

Sacred Vigil

The major advantage of having a second floor apartment on Clifton Boulevard is that it commands a view of the sidewalk. Even though his building faced Arbor Avenue, from his south windows he could see everyone who got on and off the bus that ran to downtown Cleveland. In this case, the *everyone* was the woman he knew as Rachael. His first impression of her came from her unvarying allegiance to a daily routine. Every morning from his high perch, he watched her board the No. 55 bus. He could depend upon her being at the stop near his window Monday through Friday by 7:51 a.m. when the bus arrived. For over two-and-a-half years he kept track of her unwavering schedule. For the longest time, he wondered where she went each day. He knew the bus route from the brochure supplied by the RTA. It ran east along Clifton Boulevard a block north of Public Square and then on toward Playhouse Square and Cleveland State University. When the time was right, he left his apartment before her scheduled arrival and walked west in order to get on the bus a stop ahead. That was a Tuesday, and he was quite pleased when the familiar block of red brick buildings came into view, the bus stopped and Rachael stepped up through the open doors, walking past him as she found a seat further back. He looked away as she passed, but felt a movement of air as she brushed by. She got off the bus at Ontario Street near the Justice Center. He went one stop further before disembarking. He walked back along Lakeside, but by the time he reached Ontario, Rachael had disappeared into the heart of the city. He crossed the avenue and caught the next bus back to Lakewood and home. After that, he rode the bus every Tuesday, always following the same pattern of walking west to get on ahead of her. He felt that they had a lot in common. Like him, she was a creature of unswerving habit, missing only the national holidays and, as he had noted, the special dates of the Christian calendar.

It was not so much that he loved this Rachael; in fact, it was important that he did not actually know her. It was enough to know that she was *Rachael*, a name shared with his mother and with several others whom he had admired in the past. The truth was that he had taken this very apartment so that he could maintain his sacred vigil. On a very few days, she had broken her routine, and it sent him to a near panic. Once he walked a block-and-a-half to stand on the sidewalk across from her house. He thought of a series of excuses to climb the three stone steps of the stoop to knock on the door just to see that she would answer. He thought of bringing his van around from the alley garage where he kept it parked. He could tell her that it stalled in front of her building, and could he use the phone? But he was not ready to address Rachael by name. *That will happen on a Thursday, not now*, he thought.

He always first spoke to his Rachaels on Thursdays. He had been born on a Thursday, as his mother had often told him. "You came out talking too much, even then," she often scolded.

In his heart he knew that his mother loved him deeply, but she was a stickler for detail and would have to discipline him when he let her down. He couldn't blame her. He was all she had. In the end, he was the one who had cared for her in her final moments of life. There had been a great deal of discussion at the hospital when the discharge planner suggested that she be moved to an extended care facility. He remembered his mother's gratitude at being able to stay at home when he had assured the planner that he could handle the routine of his mother's treatment regimen. A visiting nurse could check in on her, but he would have no part of a nursing home. The staff nurse at the hospital gave him a crash course in how to make sure her airway on her trach was clear. It was simply a matter of keeping a steady routine. Every two hours on the even hour he would meticulously suction the tubing according to the schedule that had been set up for him. He did not have to worry between cleanings since the ventilator to which she was attached also had an alarm which would awaken him or call him away from the television.

It was the alarm that called him in her final moments. He often thanked the buzz that had summoned him to the bedside as she passed from this life. Had it not sounded, she might have died alone in a gasping panic. He had seen the fear in her eyes as he approached the bed. It was only ten minutes before he was scheduled to suction her throat. As he waited, he saw the relief in her eyes and knew it was love. There was a rattle in her throat that seemed to bellow from deep within. Her eyes rolled back and he knew that he had seen her through the end. It was perfect in its way.

At two o'clock, he performed his scheduled duty of suctioning the trach tube. After that, he called 9-1-1. It was Thursday.

Chapter 2

Trip to Shanghai

Davis McGowan used his turn signal to indicate that he was merging into the left lane. There were orange barrels ahead on Route 2 and the idiot reflected in his driver's side mirror seemed intent on pulling even with McGowan's car at the very moment that the plastic barrels funneled all traffic into a single-lane construction zone. There didn't seem much point in going faster to try and outrun the slowly approaching car; Davis was already gaining on the semi in front of him and being threatened by the temporary signs that promised doubled fines in a construction area.

"Crazy drivers! That's another reason to say 'no'," he said aloud. He had been arguing with himself for two days. This was just the latest round. He was driving east from his home in Huron for an afternoon meeting at the Old First Church on Cleveland's Public Square.

The driver coming up behind him was now up on his bumper, but backed off when a parked State Trooper's car came into view just ahead of a hulking machine that was scraping the asphalt off the road surface. "Sure, you'll slow down for her," he commented as he passed the officer standing to the side of a white car with the winged logo of the Ohio State Police.

He had agreed to come out of retirement to take a six month stint as the interim pastor at the landmark church. A few weeks ago, he was living anonymously in Huron, Ohio, but then he was invited to speak at John Knox Church in North Olmsted. Cleveland, like most large cities, is a small town which disguises itself with a large population. In any case, a First National executive from John Knox said something in passing to a friend from Temple Israel who was attending a lunch hour meeting for the hunger coalition that was being held at Old First. In the days before it was called "networking," it was just the grapevine. The end result was that McGowan was returning. Returning to Cleveland, and returning to parish ministry, at least for a time.

In some ways, the whole prospect was frightening, and Davis knew that it was his self-doubt that gave rise to all the excuses that he could now name for something that seemed perfectly reasonable a week earlier. In all fairness, the people at Old First had dismantled his reservations one by one. He already knew that it was a one hour drive from Huron to East Ninth Street and the parking garage near Browns' Stadium. He was not as sure about traffic around the Square, but Old First had an off-street parking lot and, by agreement, the five-day commute was cut to three. On the other days, he could work from home via the Internet. He thought briefly about driving into Brookpark or Puritas and taking the Rapid Transit to the Terminal Tower. It would be the same commute that his father had employed when Davis was in high school, but there was little value in that now.

The highway system was faster and more direct than his earlier memory dictated.

The fact remained that there were a lot of personal reasons why Davis McGowan might surrender six months of his retirement to get back to the metropolitan area. It was in a moment of nostalgia that he had said, "Yes." Today, he would pick up the keys and meet the support staff. He knew from his own experience that the men and women who worked behind the scenes in churches were often the real bearers of a congregation's self-image, and the church secretary frequently served as a caregiver for the lonely and distressed.

By now Route 2 East had merged into I-90 as it sped through Sheffield and on toward Cleveland's western suburbs. All this was new to Davis. When he was growing up in North Olmsted, towns like Vermilion and Huron were way out in the country and even the trek to the downtown followed the twists and turns of city streets through Fairview Park, Rocky River, and Lakewood. Now the freeways bypassed the old neighborhoods of shops and houses that became a timeline of the city's expanse. Like the rings of a growing tree with the inner bands being the oldest, the houses of the west side radiated in rings of neighborhoods.

It was a problem faced by many of the rust belt cities. Sure, there were attempts at regentrification, and Ohio City and Tremont stood out as testimony to the success of that effort. Then again, there was Crocker Park, a shopping area in the outer growth ring that mimicked small town America. Here the parking garages and chain stores are hidden beneath a veneer of boutique storefronts and cobbled streets. It is a shopping theme park, but just a few miles away were the real neighborhoods and small shops along Detroit Avenue in Lakewood. Still, in a throwaway society, nostalgia trumps reality.

This would not be the case for McGowan. His forty-year-old memories of Cleveland would not likely serve him now. Then again, he was no longer the boy with the illusion of a future in front of him. Still, the boy stays in the man, and he turned off the interstate at Clague Road and headed north toward Lake Road. He would make this first trip to Public Square by the old paths.

Chapter 3

Patterns

Darnell Wilson straightened his tie before knocking on Captain Wakeman's office door. The gesture had become a habit that had not gone unnoticed by his co-workers who dubbed him Mr. GQ. The reality was quite different. It was not fashion sense that drove him so much as a volunteer tutor at the neighborhood center where he grew up.

"Darnell," she said, "you have a lot of ability, but you need to learn how to carry yourself better. If you dress like a punk, people will treat you like one. Now we're here in the ghetto, but we don't have to be the ghetto. I have high hopes for you."

Darnell suspected that Ms. Brown said that to all the students she worked with on reading and math, but, at the time, he knew she was talking to him. When he was in college he was all-business, and sent a personal note of thanks to Miss. Brown on the occasion of her eighty-fifth birthday. If he was Mr. GQ now, it was her doing. In any case, he stood out and moved out of the uniform ranks to become a member of the investigation team.

Still, being called to the Precinct Captain's office was always a bit tense. He knew the topic at hand. It was related to an observation that he had put forward before, and now he was being asked to argue it again. The previous times, however, his suggestions were set aside quickly but politely. Admittedly, eleven years ago he was new to the force and was just learning community policing in this precinct. The September 10th murder of a middle-aged woman didn't fit any normal category that he had been taught. She was single with no apparent romantic interests. She lived in Lakewood, had no history of prostitution, drug use, or unusual money transactions. "Sweet," "dependable," "committed friend," were the words of her co-workers. They could not imagine anyone wanting to do her harm. Their lack of imagination, however, could not undo the fact that she was found near Edgewater Park, strangled with a length of power cord from a computer game box. At the time, it seemed a strange weapon, and so it still seemed for a nine-year-old cold case.

Three years later, on September 10th, another middle-aged Lakewood woman was found strangled in the Park just inside Cleveland. This time it was a cell phone charger cord. As with the earlier homicide, this body was found around three o'clock, and, according to the coroner's office, as much as seven hours after the time of death. The victim fit the same description as the first: single, middle-aged, white female. She had no apparent enemies, and her friends knew her as warm, dependable, hard-working, and punctual.

That was the first time that Darnell voiced his concern. It was sloughed off as coincidence, but his annual review noted that he had a good memory for details. Three years later, the reoccurring bad dream again made its way into the Plain Dealer, but the media only reported a murder, and had not connected the growing string of anniversary dates. By then Darnell Wilson was a detective and Boyd Wakeman, his new captain. Wakeman didn't need to be persuaded.

"I know we must have been driving you crazy, Wilson," he said. "Three women are dead, but a three-year cycle isn't easy to verify. We're coming up on the end of another three-year period so I'm going to assume that there's a nut case out there that is going to crawl out of his hole this year on September 10th. These are cold cases, I know, but… well, the pattern is hard to write off."

"Yes Sir," agreed Darnell. He wanted to scream, "And we have lost ground on it!" but he knew that all he had earlier was his instinct, and policing was limited to the evidence-at-hand and the taxpayers' dollars.

"I've called in a profiler to work with you, but I can't really promise you much else. If we are right, a little more than a month from now, on September 10th, we'll be looking at another corpse."

Darnell noticed the "we" in the Captain's remarks, but held his silence.

"This is going to be an over-and-above assignment, Darnell. You know what I mean?"

"Yes, Sir. You want me to figure this out on my own time."

Wakeman smiled. "You're a true believer, aren't you?"

"Sir?"

"Justice," offered Boyd. "Not like the movies where we're the bad guys."

"No, Sir. Not at all like the movies."

"Keep me informed. I've given the files to Megan Sorento; she's the profiler that's been assigned. Right now it'll be just you two. I'd prefer to keep it quiet. The word 'serial' has a way of creating a mob scene and a nightmare for the politicians."

"Is that all, Sir?"

"Wilson, this isn't a reprimand. You're a damn good cop, and I've just dumped a lot in front of you."

"I know, Sir. I appreciate your confidence; I just have some work to do."

For the second time, Boyd Wakeman, the gray-haired veteran smiled. "Well, at least let me shake your hand!"

Darnell Wilson wasn't sure what to do, but an open hand was extended in his direction. He took it before he could think.

"Darnell, I've asked you to be low-keyed on this, but keep me in the loop. I don't want any surprises. And, if you need anything, well, I'll do what I can."

It had not been the meeting that he had anticipated. When Wilson left the Captain's office he felt different. He was an eleven-year career officer, but he felt like a rookie detective on his first case. At least he was not alone on this; the profiler might give him some ideas. Otherwise, he was not quite sure where to begin.

Chapter 4

Old First

Davis had been instructed to park in the lot across the street just south and west of the church building. The lot attendant asked how long he would be and, as instructed, he replied that he had a meeting at "Old First."

"Then take the ticket with you and they'll validate your parking." The man handed a time-stamped manila receipt to McGowan. "Just pull into any of the open spaces."

For August, the temperature was comfortable. It was a day of blue skies and a northwest breeze off the lake. Davis noted that Public Square had shrunk from the greater dimensions of his memory. Maybe it was just that the newer buildings presented a larger skyline. In the sixties, the Erieview project wrested away dominance from the Terminal Tower which had stood proudly as the guardian of tradition. Now both seemed crowded out by new growth. Still, all the older pieces were in place: the Soldiers' and Sailors' Monument, the open space around the Moses Cleaveland monument, and, nestled in the shadow of Society Bank, the Old First Presbyterian Church.

These were all vestiges of an older Cleveland when steel was the basis of wealth, and ore was brought to the mills in the bellies of Great Lakes' freighters which offloaded mountains of iron on the banks of the Cuyahoga. Now the most famous of the freighters, the *William G. Mather*, was docked as a museum near the Rock-and-Roll Hall of Fame. It had been named for the heir of Samuel Mather whose fortune in the iron industry led to the founding of a bank in 1849, the Society for Savings. Its ten-story building, once the tallest between New York City and Chicago, had lost that honor long ago. Along with it went the name. Society Bank was no longer "Society Bank" in spite of what the bronze plaque near the cornerstone stated. In the morphology of corporate America it had gone through a series of names and lost its "Society" status under newer identities like Ameritrust and now, Key Corp. Time had unmasked the permanence that companies tout in their annual reports. Even the Terminal Tower, on the south side of the Square, had become "Tower City" in one of Cleveland's realignments. McGowan always felt that this was a very livable place, a place that, unfortunately, had grown expert at shooting itself in the foot. Even the early mapmakers messed up, and now poor Moses, the surveyor who had laid out the site, looked down from his monument on the city that had trouble spelling his last name.

Only Old First seemed the same, a symbol of constancy in a city of change. To passersby the imagery might be lost, but to church leaders, being the conservators of faith is a two-edged sword. Often "constancy" is viewed as a synonym for "static," and, even among dwindling numbers, people can confuse *holding the line* with *faithfulness*. Some urban congregations tried to survive by merely circling the wagons in a secular world as the new towers of worship grew around them. Still, the homeless walked the streets or broke into the refuge of boarded-up houses.

Inner-city congregations sit at the intersection of poverty and politics. Old First had a long rich history, sitting here on Public Square. At one time, its steeple was a high landmark mirroring the Terminal Tower; now it seemed a thorny spike among the giants. McGowan laughed at the thought. Long ago, his grandmother had told him the story of how a thorny plant saved Scotland. During a stealthy night attack, a enemy soldier stepped barefoot on a thistle. When he yelled out, the Scots under Robert the Bruce were quick to arms and victory. In a new age where religious expression seems a remnant of an arcane past, Old First is a community which could cry out against the expediencies of money and power. At least that was McGowan's hope.

He made his way east past the stone steps that led up to the great golden oak doors that faced the square. He turned left on Ontario and found the weekday entry doors. The glass door was locked, but a laminated sign pointed toward an intercom. Davis pushed the button.

"Hello, may I help you?" came a woman's friendly voice.

"I'm Davis McGowan," he answered, "I have an appointment to meet Fred Reynolds here at 1:00." The latch clicked.

"Come in, Dr. McGowan." Davis pulled at the door which opened on a wide vestibule. Straight ahead and up a small flight of steps was a long counter which divided the entrance hall from an open office area. A woman stood as he approached.

"Dr. Reynolds just called to say he will be delayed a few minutes at the University. Would you like to come into the office and wait? Can I get you a cup of coffee or anything?"

Davis smiled. "You're good," he said. The woman blushed a little then caught McGowan's expression. "I'm Davis," he said. "Thank you for letting me in."

"I'm Colleen McQuisten," she answered. "It's my job to open the door. Besides, I believe you are my new boss."

"It's nice to meet a believer," he said extending his hand. "But I have to warn you that it's always been my belief that the person who opens the door usually knows more about what's going on than the boss."

McQuisten smiled. "A man who understands me," she quipped. It was, perhaps, a risky comment to include in the first exchange with a new supervisor, but it just seemed to slip out naturally before it could be measured. "Sorry," she hastened to add.

"Don't be," said Davis. "I always look for a sense of humor, and I think you have one. We'll probably get along fine."

"Would you like to come see your office?"

"If it's okay, Colleen, I'd like to go into the sanctuary. I was here about forty years ago, and I'd like to refresh my memory."

"Sure, Dr. McGowan, it's just down the hall. I'll send Dr. Reynolds down to meet you when he gets here."

"I don't know how staff dynamics have been here before. In front of company we may need the 'Dr. McGowan' talk, but I tend toward first names within the work group. You can call me 'Davis'."

"Well, that's the way it has been around here with most of the pastors."

"Most of the pastors? How long have you been working here?"

"Thirty-five years next month."

Davis turned to go toward the sanctuary, "but who's counting?"

"Be sure and stay on this level," she called after him. "There are stairs near the front door, but the alarm system will trip if you go down."

"Good to know!" said Davis, "You're already looking out for me, thanks." He didn't realize how this lighthearted exchange had relieved Colleen's anxiety about a new supervisor. McGowan's own relief came from the immediate recognition that at least one of the regular staff had a commitment to this place. The others probably did as well. But what sort of place was this anyway? He had forgotten about security systems within buildings. The year he spent at College Hill in Dayton had broken him of his habit of wandering around the building as an escape from his desk. There, as here, motion detectors would shout out any embarrassing lapses. He did not intend to wander in any case. He did not need to.

This moment alone in the sanctuary brought him full circle in his career. He looked up at the vaulted ceiling. Now it struck him that he was looking into the deep rounded bilges of an old sailing vessel. Forty years ago, before he had taken to sailing, the dark oak beams seemed the mark of a high-steeple church. The person in this pulpit would be poised to accomplish something worthwhile. Davis laughed to himself, "I thought I might save the world," he said to no one.

His career had sent him to larger congregations in different cities. He had served on the highest councils of his denomination, but had grown to know the truth. His CEO friends would say, "There's no view from the top." He knew that all the advances and successes of parish life would never count for anything when standing beside a father telling his children that their mother died while they were asleep.

"Are you lost?" said Fred Reynolds, who had entered the sanctuary. Davis turned to greet him.

"Lost? Not this time," he said. "I sat in this room a long time ago. I was in college and had to wait here while the Candidates' Committee sharpened their questions to see if I was cut out to be a pastor." Davis' eyes went back to the high vaulted ceiling and down the woodwork of the chancel where a rainbow of color washed in through the Tiffany stained glass windows.

"Obviously, you passed."

His emotions were running deep, but he spoke his usual lighthearted retort. "Nah, I basically faked it and was given a free ride. I suppose that's not the best thing to admit to a guy who has just offered me a job." McGowan's first impression of Fred Reynolds during the interview was all-business. He had been introduced as Professor Reynolds from Cleveland State, and he spent most of the interview with his eyes shifting between the pages of Davis' dossier and over his half glasses when he asked a direct question.

"Are you telling me that you faked your credentials?" His manner matched McGowan's banter.

"Not on purpose, it just sort of happened! I just wasn't examined very closely."

Reynolds' puzzled look was an invitation to continue.

"I'm sure you understand what I mean. I've graded a lot of student papers and have come to the conclusion that if I were a student with an average paper, I'd want my professor to read it right after the worst paper in the pile. You know what I mean?"

"We've all been there," agreed Reynolds. "You're so relieved to read something that makes a little sense, and you're right, I bet the grade gets higher."

"Well," continued McGowan, "it was kinda like that. Years after my meeting here with the Candidates' Committee, I was scheduled to come before the entire

Presbytery as part of my trials for ordination. I was to be publicly questioned by the whole assembly. This was back in '72, and I followed a candidate that sparked a little controversy… no, he nearly started a floor-fight over his answers to the questions from the delegates."

"And you were on deck."

"It was up at Fairmont, on The Heights. I was sitting outside the sanctuary waiting my turn at being questioned. Finally, my turn came to stand before the inquisition. I read my statement of faith and the moderator opened the floor for questions. There was silence. I think they were all worn out. A motion was made and my ordination was passed without a single answer on my part."

"Your lucky day, then."

"Always felt a little cheated. I was twenty-three, about to graduate from Princeton, and loaded for bear!"

"Then it was *their* lucky day! You probably scared them. I think you are going to fit in well here at Old First," said Fred.

"I hope so," answered Davis. "As I've gotten older I've lost some of my patience with the obstructionists. I used to be diplomatic, but now I just want to cut to the chase. Beth says that I just don't tolerate fools any longer."

"I should hope not," said Reynolds.

Chapter 5

Night Shift

Richard Kosten took a long drag from his cigarette and blew the white smoke through the crack he had opened in the driver's side window of the van. The clock on the dashboard read 10:05, and already the cashier from the Wallace Pharmacy had been to the door several times to unlock and relock to let late customers out of the store.

This was a part of the job he really enjoyed, especially when patrons rushing to make a last minute run to the pharmacy came up short when unmoving automatic doors threatened to rearrange their faces.

At a quarter after the hour, a black-haired clerk in a blue vest came to the glass door and waved at the van. This was his signal. He inhaled the last of his smoke, opened the door, and stepped out of the vehicle. As he walked past the grill, he looked back into the store and made a sweeping gesture as if inviting the woman at the window to join him. Instead, she stuck out her tongue and thrust a hip to the side which revealed a pink bulge just above her low-rise jeans. They both laughed and Richard waved her off.

"Make me do all the work," he called out loud enough to be heard through the insulated doors.

She slid the door open. "Hey, I'm at the end of my shift. I could go home now if I didn't have to hang around to protect the store from the floor cleaner guy!"

"And I thought you loved me?"

"I do love you; after all, you are my Dickybird, but there's still gum on the floor in aisle nine and some angel with black soles was burning rubber in the toy aisle."

"Nix the Dickybird stuff; besides didn't you get married?"

"I waited for you to ask, but a girl can't wait forever."

A blue-shirted EXA came round an end-unit and stepped toward the door. The banter stopped. "Heather, why don't you start pulling outdates in cough and cold," he said. "Hello, Richard, the floors are a bit rough."

"No problem, Mr. Wozniak, I'll take care of it." Richard winked at Heather, who was turning to head to the back wall where the over-the-counter cold remedies were kept. She would be reading the expiration dates on the packages, pulling the older stock to the front, and placing a yellow sticky dot on products that would expire within two months. It was not her favorite job. It was no one's favorite job, but it kept her motivated in her course work at the community college.

Richard returned to the van, pulling open the sliding side door, and positioning a metal ramp to lower the stainless steel box that was his floor buffer. He grabbed the stuff-bag that contained the disposable gloves and booties that were a part of his maintenance routine. He patted the back pocket of his faded jeans to make sure his scraper was still there. Once in the store, he went to work on the gum using a flat-bladed putty knife to scrape the floor. He walked through every aisle stopping only to remove the black heel marks with a soft cloth that he dipped in solvent. He gave a low whistle as he approached the cough and cold section. Heather looked up with a smile of recognition.

"Sexy," he whispered. Nothing else was spoken, but they both knew that the flirting would resume once Wozniak went back to the office. Heather was a looker, he thought. He'd never thought of asking her out, but now that she was married he could still be her friend. *Maybe a friend with benefits,* he thought as he looked back at her.

In the alcove near the pharmacy counter he started stacking the chairs. The "angel" who left the skid marks obviously had short legs and hyperactivity. Swinging feet had managed to put racing stripes under every chair but one. *That's where Mommy sat,* thought Richard. *Somebody should have smacked her for not watching her kid!*

Once the chairs were out of the way, he brought in the stainless steel sheathed buffer to bring the floor surface back to its clinically pure sheen. Overseeing the process was a poster image of the head pharmacist. Beneath the photo of a young slender black woman in a white lab coat was her name and college: "Rochelle Mayberry, Pharm D, Ohio Northern."

"Too young, not curvy enough… sorry," he said as he saluted the image. Heather was more his type, but she was ready to leave and he had to buff out the toy aisle.

He positioned himself toward the front of the store to have one last flirt before she went home for the night.

"Goodnight, Dickybird," she volunteered as he focused on a nonexistent scuff along a baseboard.

"Going home without me?"

"You should have made your move sooner," she cooed.

"Never too late," he answered. "If that new husband of yours doesn't satisfy, well, I'd be willing to show you how I can really wax and buff!"

Heather blushed. She liked Richard and would have welcomed a chance to date him, but he had never acted this explicit before. Maybe he liked women who were married and inaccessible. Maybe he knew that she wasn't. "Now Dickybird, what would your Rachael say if she knew you were hitting on a cashier?"

"She'd be cool with it."

Chapter 6

Megan Sorento

Darnell Wilson was not a regular visitor to the FBI headquarters on Lakeside Drive so he didn't want to count on being recognized as he approached the security checkpoint with its metal detectors. The better part of valor, he thought, was to not carry. Besides, it was his day off and as far as the Lakewood Police were concerned, his meeting with Megan Sorento wasn't happening in any official capacity.

He had done the correct thing. None of the faces were familiar as he emptied the contents of his pockets into a container that had an uncanny resemblance to a pet bowl.

"I see the budget cuts have reached over into Cleveland."

"Huh?" said the stocky brunette who was stirring the dish before placing it on the conveyor.

"The high security dog dishes that you've been issued. Petsmart?"

The woman gave him the eye, and Darnell wondered if he had crossed the demilitarized zone. Then a grin broke free as she obviously judged him friend not foe.

"Nothing but the best for the taxpayer," she said. "Where do you serve?"

"If it's that obvious that I'm a cop, I'll have to try harder," he quipped. "Lakewood."

"No, you look fine. It's your shield. The scanner really liked it!"

"That's a relief. It's bad enough to have to tell a date that you're a cop, much less have them see it on your face as you're making the approach."

"Are you off duty? Or are you going to show us your arsenal?"

"I'm a civilian today. Strictly pleasure, well not exactly. I'm meeting Megan Sorento."

The guard gave him that look again. "So it's a date?"

"Not a date, more like an arranged meeting," said Darnell.

"That's good," said the woman, "but you must be some kind of date risk if you have to meet her in a secure building. Most people choose a public place. Ever hear of a coffee shop? You do know that she's packing so you're entering at your own risk."

They were both laughing and a brother who had been standing near the opposite wall came to join the discussion.

"I think that you've gotten the wrong idea," Wilson confessed. "This meeting is pure business."

"Too bad for you, then. How would you describe Megan Sorento, Eddie?"

The uniformed guard made a sizzling sound that ended with the word "hot" and the disclaimer, "but I didn't say that and don't tell my wife!"

The party ended when a petite, olive-skinned woman rounded the corner. Her handsome features were masked by an air of determination and the glint of steel in her deep brown eyes.

"And here she is," said the security guard. Brother went quickly back to the other side of the corridor. "Ms. Sorento, there's a man here to see you."

"Darnell? I'm glad you could meet today." Wilson scrambled to recover the items from the dog dish and, with that, the two were headed into the depths of the building. "Boyd Wakeman has told me a little about the situation, but I think we need to set out what we know."

"Did he also tell you that the case is 'off the record' for now?"

"Yes, that's why he asked me to help. He knew that he could get me to volunteer some time."

"So, it's your day off, too?"

"Yep, and I can't tell you how happy I am to face the walls of justice."

"It does feel like a prison sometimes," offered Wilson. "It's tough to work out a private life."

"They give you a private life in Lakewood? Any openings over there for me?" Megan's demeanor burst open with a smile.

"I haven't found one, but I'm hopeful. The badge isn't a chick magnet."

"Doesn't work on guys either," she confessed as the lift doors opened.

Megan's office was housed on one of the upper floors, and the two were silent as they watched the red digital numbers cycle through the various levels.

Darnell should have expected it, but was still surprised when he got off the elevator and found himself facing a second checkpoint.

"This is Darnell Wilson from the Lakewood PD," said Sorento to the uniformed guard who stepped toward the couple. "He's not carrying."

"That's what they all say." Darnell couldn't tell if the guard's comment was in good humor or deadly serious. He decided to err on the side of caution and held off on any banter. You don't want to appear as a smart-mouthed stranger in a department where every desk was occupied by a service revolver and someone schooled in the art of deadly force. It was a good decision.

After a pat-down, the two walked into a large open office with rank on rank of desks, most in use by men and women intent on their work.

"Sorry about that," said Megan as they approached an empty desk, "relaxing security is not a current prerogative. Seems like it should be unnecessary given the fact that most of our cases are white collar crime."

Darnell was looking out the north-facing windows and didn't seem to notice. "You've got quite a view of the lake from here."

"It was even better when we were on the top two floors of the Federal Building. There, we were thirty floors up and had the best view in town. Still, this is pretty good! It makes up for the lack of privacy."

"I see you're enjoying your day off." The comment came from a thirty-something man who was walking toward them along the aisle of desks. Darnell noticed that the crisp white shirt had French cuffs with ebony links.

"You know how it is, Bruce," answered Megan, "crime doesn't yada yada. This is Darnell Wilson from Lakewood. Darnell, this is Bruce McClelland." As he stepped forward to take the agent's outstretched hand, he wondered how many introductions the day would bring and how many of these names he had to commit to memory.

"Thinking of becoming a Fed?" asked McClelland.

The question caught Wilson off-balance. The thought had never occurred to him.

"This is just local business," Megan interrupted. "In fact, I'm not even here today. It's a favor to an old friend. If it has to go into the record, put it down as interagency cooperation with a local PD."

"Homeland Security it is, then," said the agent putting a finger to his lips as if signaling a secret. "Have fun!"

"Loads," bandied Sorento who then indicated an open seat across from a desk. She sat first, and Wilson knew he had entered her "office".

"Bruce is my immediate supervisor," she offered.

"Seems like an okay guy."

"If you like dedicated, bright, and efficient," said Megan.

"Are you two…"

"Did I mention that he's married, two kids, and one on the way?"

"You left that part out." In spite of the surroundings, Darnell felt comfortable here. He didn't give it much thought one way or the other as to whether it was the rarified air of dedication to service or Megan Sorento whose steely first impression turned out to be a well-honed disguise.

"Boyd says that you suspect that you have a serial killer on your hands." The statement brought Wilson back to reality.

"It's just a hunch. We've have three murders exactly three years apart to the day. Same victim profile, same form of strangulation."

"Different ligatures."

Darnell wondered how much Megan already knew. She answered before he could form any questions.

"Boyd sent over your reports. Forgive me, but I needed to depose the witness to make sure the story hadn't changed." This was the third time that she had referred to Wakeman by his first name, a familiarity that he did not share.

"Captain Wakeman told me that he had sent you information, but I wasn't sure how much. Sounds like you are completely up-to-speed."

"Well, he wanted to give me some time to make up a profile. The three-year gap between murders is a puzzle. It could be a number of things, some harder to trace than others. For example, there may be other victims; maybe even in other cities, but he only is in Cleveland every three years on that date."

"I did some checking for other killings on that date and couldn't find any exact matches," offered Darnell. "Oh, there were plenty of murders, but not single, white, middle-aged women strangled with a cord and with no probable suspects, domestic altercations and so forth."

"Then I suspect that the three years is part of a ritual cycle."

"A ritual?"

"There are a lot of motivating factors for people who become serial murderers. Sometimes it is a reenactment of some trauma that plays over and over again in the mind of the killer. It can be set off by any number of things, a sound, a smell, a strong memory. Almost anything can be the trigger. I suspect that the person perpetrating these crimes correlates September 10th with the culmination of a three-year period. That's why so much time elapses between murders."

"And why it took nine years to find a pattern?"

"Exactly," continued Sorento, "but sometimes there's no apparent pattern at all. The killer seizes on any opportunity that presents itself. Missing Persons reports come in, but people go missing all the time and there's nothing to link them."

"Then a body shows up like the Imperial Avenue murders on the East Side," offered Wilson.

"Tell me about it. We did some of the background work here in this office. The case was solved in a matter of hours. It's just that the crime went undetected for a long time. Anthony Sowell, the man accused, didn't have a car. He took the bus everywhere, but it looks like in four years he killed eleven women in his home. Well, you know about the case. It even made the BBC. Great publicity for Cleveland, huh?"

"In Lakewood we actually felt sorry for the metro cops. They had to explain why they didn't even know that eleven black women were missing. Of course that wasn't true. There just weren't any connections. Sowell was a registered sex offender who kept all the rules. The women who complained about him always described him as their 'boyfriend' so the protests never rose above domestic disputes. Neighbors complained about foul odors and the city was on the spot to clean drains over and over again. Nobody ever thought that what they were smelling was decomposing bodies. Why would they?"

"And the poor guy who ran the butcher shop next door!" said Megan. "Every complaint about the odor sent the Board of Health to his shop. Everyone was trying to fix a little piece of a problem. They just didn't see the real problem, and at least eleven people were murdered. They were crimes of opportunity. He allegedly lured them in, and they went willingly. Like your case, they ended up strangled."

Darnell and Megan sat in silence for a moment. Wilson's gaze went out to the lake where a white sail was ghosting along the horizon. "Ever wonder what it's like to be out there on one of those?"

Megan followed Wilson's gaze. "On a sailboat?"

"Yes. They seem so smooth and quiet."

"Sometimes they are. Sometimes what you see at a distance isn't what it's like at all. That boat could be beating against every oncoming wave, but we just see a white silhouette."

"Sounds like you've been out there some."

"My brother was a sailor. Crewed on Wednesday night races out of the sailing club. He took me out a couple of times when he could borrow a boat."

"Is he still around? I'd like to try it."

Megan hesitated. "He died ten years ago."

"I'm sorry. I didn't know."

"How could you? He was killed in an accident. But that was a long time ago. Nothing would please me more than to be out there with him. Sometimes I walk down by the water just to feel close to him. He liked the lake." The sound of Beethoven's *Ode to Joy* pulled them out of the silence that had overtaken them. They turned to see an agent two stations away pulling a cell phone from his jacket pocket.

"Anyway," began Megan, "I think we are dealing with a different sort of killer, and if he has only had three victims, then you've caught him early. The Bureau doesn't classify murders as 'serial' until there are three victims."

"That's the problem, we haven't caught anyone yet. We just know about them."

"Well it looks like we are dealing with some sort of ritualized pattern. He doesn't seem to be very creative or secretive about hiding the body. I don't think that there's evidence that the people were killed at Edgewater, but it's where he wants the victims to be found. For whatever reason, it makes sense to him. He's probably commemorating some event, not just a date."

"That's why three years rather than every September 10th," acknowledged Darnell. "You said 'he,' you think it's a male?"

"Yes, probably a white male, mid-twenties. Lives close to where he grew up. Detroit corridor, near West Side, Ohio City, Lakewood– somewhere in that area. He's right on the edge of different jurisdictions so coordination between police departments will take some high level authorization."

"Which ain't going to happen," said Wilson.

Megan smiled. "That's pretty easy to deduce, isn't it? How many overtime hours has your department approved for this investigation?"

It was Darnell's turn to smile. "Same as the Feds. We're both sitting here on our day off."

"Boyd Wakeman shares our concerns and is willing to let us work it out on our own," said Sorento.

"So this is the life of an FBI profiler?" said Wilson, looking around the room.

"Did Boyd say that I was a profiler?"

"Yes, and I was impressed that my suspicions ranked high enough to get the attention of the Feds."

Megan smiled. "That's why he's the Captain, but he knows better. On TV there are people in the FBI called profilers, but in real life there's no such job description. The high level stuff is done in Washington by

Supervisory Special Agents at the National Center for the Analysis of Violent Crime. Someday I hope to get a shot at that level. I studied behavioral science and forensics for just that, but mostly I go through papers to build cases against corruption and look out over the lake."

"Maybe he thought this sort of unofficial case would help?"

Sorento looked away for a long moment. "We have little to go on in this case," she began abruptly, "The forensics are almost non-existent. From what I see there's really only one print from twelve years ago, but no match from the Bureau of Criminal Investigation. Have you run that print recently? A lot of data would have come in in the last few years."

Wilson shook his head.

"Well, I am making some major leaps here, but this is how it looks to me," Megan continued. "The killings began almost twelve years ago. My hunch is that the murderer was young–high school. He was into video games. Back then, it was kids who played those games. The fact is that they never grew out of them and that's why so many boring men play them today. Are you a video gamer?"

"No," said Darnell.

"Good," she said without missing a beat. "He has a love/hate relationship with his mother. He kills her every three years, for some reason. The date is something important, his birthday, her birthday, the day his father walked out."

"His father?"

"There's a lot of rage here. Abandonment is a big theme. His victims are white, so he is white. The victims are more mature, the age of his mother when the murders began. He's probably still in the area and apparently has no problem getting close enough to these women to slip something around their necks. He seems like an ordinary guy, maybe boyish enough to invoke some maternal instincts."

"Maybe this is pointless," argued Wilson. "Say he was sixteen when he started this mess… he'd be twenty-eight by now. Wouldn't something click? He'd get a job or go to school, you know, move on."

"He's stuck in a cycle. He can't move on. People who are deeply wounded like this never get over it. He's probably keeping to himself, not drawing attention, living off a low-level job, and waiting for September 10th."

Darnell paused to consider Megan's last comment. "Seems pretty harsh," he added. "People do change."

"Not very often, or at least not without some sort of intervention. These people have already figured out how to handle the demons that haunt them. They kill, and you can bet he's giving it a lot of thought right now."

Chapter 7

Thirty-five

Davis spent the majority of his thirty-one years of pastoral ministry in five congregations, and he knew that the first few weeks in a new position were critical. Entering a new church was akin to landing in an alien world. In the first days he would be bombarded with calls from people interested in making a connection with the "new guy." The problem for the pastor is sorting through the smiles and handshakes without the advantage of knowing the dynamics of the parish. As with any group of people, congregations are divided into subsets, each with intersecting circles of influence and personal loyalties. Sometimes competing interests for limited resources create undercurrents of resentment and hostility. In particular, he recalled one volunteer who would not share the password to the computer which controlled the building's thermostats. McGowan always wanted to believe that the man had the church's financial interests at heart, but suspected that the real issue was more likely related to a sadistic streak that revealed itself in laughter when the staff asked if the winter setback temperature had to be as low as fifty-five degrees. At 7:30 in the morning, the thermostats would signal sixty-five degrees. On average the building recovered one degree an hour, so by 3:30, when it switched back to the night setting, the offices had reached sixty-three degrees and dropped back to sixty-one by 5:00 quitting time. Of course, like any organization an informal management structure emerged and staff members had an arsenal of small heaters that went under desks and were carried home each night. The war went on until Ebenezer Scrooge's term on the governing board ended and an energy audit revealed that no money was ever saved by such false economy.

In the first weeks it always fell to a new pastor to try and get the proper name tags on Sister Teresa, Martin Luther King, Jr., Albert Schweitzer, Uncle Ebenezer, and Lobelia Sackville-Baggins. He watched the staff as they were pulled in many different directions, and like all large churches, Davis saw that there were congregations within the congregation. The education program, the music program, and the social outreach projects all pulled against the center and vied for a share of the budget. In staff meetings, McGowan felt the divisions as Donna Adams, Alistair Montgomery, and Sarah Jane O'Neil protected the sacred turf of education, arts, and social justice. In public, cordiality ruled the day, but one by one, in private, each confessed their concerns about the other. All the undercutting was in stark contrast to the fact that at the center of this three-ringed circus was Colleen McQuisten, the ringmaster.

His first impression of her had been correct. She monitored the door and coordinated the calendar in such a way that the higher-ups filled in all the boxes without stepping on each other. McGowan was pretty sure that the whole management process was under the radar and even beneath consciousness. It had been a moment of serendipity when, on his first day, he found that McQuisten was approaching a thirty-fifth anniversary.

His plan grew out of a few well-placed suggestions, and pulled the staff together in a rare moment of devious cooperation. By Friday, everyone on the staff was already complaining that the very next week each, in their own way, was going to suffer the "Wednesday from hell!" Colleen heard all the details. Alistair Montgomery had been co-opted to intervene in a dispute at the Church of the Covenant which was trying to decide on the future of their massive pipe organ. It was payback time, he explained, for all the musical scores he had borrowed over the years.

Donna Adams, the educator, was scheduled for her annual performance review. The Personnel Committee had come up with the cockeyed idea of meeting over lunch at John Q's Steakhouse right next to the church. "Like I'll be able to eat and enjoy myself," she said, exasperated. "Why don't they just put me out of my misery here at the church and give me a gift certificate and I'll take my husband to dinner?"

"I can't imagine that they are going to give you a bad review," argued Colleen, "not in a public restaurant." But Donna didn't seem consoled.

When the "Wednesday from hell" finally came, Colleen relished the quiet of an office nearly emptied of staff. Only McGowan was back in his study, probably working on a sermon. The serenity was shattered when the phone rang and a nearly frantic Donna Adams was on the line.

"Colleen, I'm next door and I realized that I left a folder on my desk. I can't believe it, how stupid!"

"Calm down, Donna. I'll bring it out to the Ontario Street entrance. You can meet me at the door."

"You don't understand!" said Adams. "They already think I'm a ditz, and now I have to tell them that I left the one file they wanted back at the office. Colleen, I'm calling from the women's room!"

"I'll have to ask Davis to cover the phones."

"That's okay, he'll understand. It's right on top of my desk. It has a pink post-it that says 'DON'T FORGET'."

"I'll find it, and I'll be right there!" She hung up the phone. The manila folder was just where she said and clearly labeled. She stuck her head through the open door of McGowan's office. "Donna is having a minor crisis and I have to leave the building for a few. Would you listen for the phone?"

"She's just next door. Is there something that I can do?"

"No, she's waiting in the restroom."

Davis exploded into laughter. "Not a job for a man!"

Colleen caught the humor, but didn't let go of her urgency. "Well, I have to run an errand of mercy. Never thought Donna was ditzy, but there's new evidence," she said holding up the folder with its blazing pink flag. Davis followed her out to the open office area and watched as she nimbly took the steps down to the glass entry doors.

When the door eased closed, McGowan made his confession. "We got you Colleen McQuisten, and you have no clue!" A figure appeared on the street side of the door and Davis was there to let Katherine Shafer into the building.

"Right on cue," he said.

"I saw the victim leave," she answered. "You go ahead, I know the drill here."

"Thanks, Doc," and he was out the door and headed toward John Q's Steakhouse. In less than five minutes he was opening the door to the sports bar. There was a lot of commotion from beyond the dark wood panels and brass railings that separated a central eating area from the main dining room. Davis made his way toward the voices and laughter. Colleen stood on the raised dais facing a long row of joined tables. Donna Adams stood next to her, either for moral support or to cut off a hasty retreat. Donna turned and saw McGowan's approach.

"And here is the instigator of all your troubles!" she boomed. Colleen turned toward Davis.

"It was really very easy, Colleen. I simply said that you had been here thirty-five years, and everyone insisted on getting in on the celebration. Guess you just can't help it; they love you."

With this the people around the tables broke out in applause. Davis looked around the group. The church staff members were there: "Jenks" Jenkens, Bob Craig, Sarah Jane O'Neil, and Alistair Montgomery.

Additionally, the membership was represented by Fred Reynolds and a number of others. Among them was an older man, probably ten years McGowan's senior. He wore a Roman collar and Davis presumed him to be Monsignor Fitzowen from St. Luke's in Lakewood where McQuisten belonged.

The tears running down Colleen's face made Davis wonder if this was such a good idea, but she turned to him and mouthed the words, "Thank you."

"You're just getting what you deserve," he answered. He was suddenly aware that a man had quietly walked up to his side.

"Dr. McGowan?" the man began, "I am the manager here and want to welcome you to Johnny Q's. Just so you know, on parties this large we automatically include a 15% gratuity with the bills even though we are giving separate checks."

"That's fine," agreed Davis. "I know it makes a lot of extra work for the server."

"In this case it doesn't matter so much. Turns out that your Ms. McQuisten is famous among our staff, or at least with Rachel. She's our most experienced server, and when I told them that we had a large group coming in, they all rolled their eyes."

"Usually means trouble, doesn't it?"

"Usually, but when I explained that it was an appreciation lunch for the secretary at Old First, Rachel stepped right up. Turns out they have been friends since high school in Lakewood."

"Turns out that Cleveland really is a small town, isn't it?" offered McGowan.

"Well, word does tend to get around; I don't think your guest of honor had a clue though." They both looked at the delight on the faces as Colleen worked her way round the tables of the enclosed space.

"Tell you what," said Davis. "I will be paying for Colleen's lunch. Put an extra thirty dollars on my tab. Sounds like your Rachel deserves recognition too."

"Very good, sir, and you are right!" With that, he retreated somewhere toward the podium at the front entrance while greeting guests at tables enroute.

Chapter 8

Night Visions

"You must learn not to cry! You're such a baby! What man wants to have a baby for a son! No wonder your father left. I would have too, but I got stuck!"

Richard Kosten woke with a start at the piercing voice that called from his memory. Even awake, he could hear it roll across the room. He could still see the impression of his mother's fist in the pillow next to his head.

"That could have been your face," she taunted. He was crying again, or still.

She was drunk. "She really loves me very much," he said to himself like a calming mantra. A part of him believed it, and another part suspected that the alcohol was making her speak the truth of which she'd repent in sobriety. She was never a remorseful drunk.

Still, she had only hit him in the face twice. The second time the school nurse phoned home, but he did his part and explained how he hit an end table while jumping off the couch. "You know boys," she said in a sweet voice when she picked him up after school.

After that, hitting was confined to bare buttocks in the nightly ritual of his becoming a man. "Men who show weakness don't make it in this world," she would say. "Your father thought you were weak. That's why he left."

The rant was well-known to Richard. He could speak the next word before it came from his mother's mouth. "And he left on my birthday," she would say. "You were three and should have outgrown those silly tears. He knew you were becoming weak, and he walked. But you aren't weak, are you?"

"No, Mother."

"Why?"

"Because you care about me and you make me strong."

"Yes, I do care about you. And one day, your father will meet you as a man and he will know that he was wrong to leave us like he did. You have learned to endure, to not cry like a baby at a little pain. Come here!"

Until he was fourteen, he always came to her. He had read the common parenting books about spanking, and the warnings to never strike a child in anger. His mother was never angry. It was just as she said, enduring pain was a sign of strength, and he had become strong.

Fourteen was the turning point, however. She had decided that the Ping-pong paddle was no longer effective in the daily ritual, but he would prove his strength. He towered over her, and stepping into her space, he took the paddle and flung it like a Frisbee. It struck the drywall with such force that it sliced through the chalky paper. The maple handle stuck out of the wall like the grip of an ice pick.

She did not ever strike him again, but she did visit his bed as he slept and pummeled his pillow to remind him of her power and his weakness. He thanked her, but fantasized pushing his dresser against the door, or catching her in a snare when she came to him in the dark.

There came a time they reached an understanding. It did not come about through words, but through her sense of his growing power. "I could kill you," he would say, "but you are my mother, and that wouldn't be right."

Chapter 9

In the Field

Megan and Darnell had agreed to meet at Edgewater Park to walk through the prior murders, or at least observe the final locations where the bodies were discovered. In each case, the victim was found in the trunk of her own car. The actual physical evidence was sparse and investigators had surmised that the driver had not only worn gloves, but also disposable shoe coverings.

"Hospital booties?" Megan asked.

"Appears that way. They found unusual blue polyethylene fibers on the floor mats around the accelerator."

"These cases didn't fail for lack of trying, did they?"

"We had a lot of people looking," answered Darnell. "The crimes crossed jurisdictions. The bodies were dumped here at Edgewater in Cleveland, but the crimes all led back to garages in Lakewood. There was a partial print, too back at the first case–on the video game power cord. No match."

"Are you sure?" Wilson turned toward Megan in time to see a swallowed-the-canary smile appear on her face. He wondered if she ever had a day when she only looked good, but this was business and he shook it out of his mind. If he looked too long into those deep brown eyes, he would get totally disoriented.

"You have something?"

"Nothing very helpful. But a matching print was taken off a counter at a Wallace Pharmacy. It's a John Doe. Somebody jumped the counter to try to snatch some Percocet and Vicodin. They took every print near the register and tried to match them up with the surveillance video."

"And?"

"Like I said, 'nothing.' On the video, they watched the perp make his leap and it was away from the place where they had lifted the prints. All we know is that your guy was in Wallace's playing around in places where most customers don't usually touch." She added, "The pharmacy staff was eliminated."

It was Darnell's turn to smile. "You are always one step ahead of me."

"I keep waiting for you to catch up!"

Was she flirting? Maybe not. "Does anyone go in the pharmacy after hours? Housekeeping?" As soon as the words were out of his mouth, he wanted to catch them and throw them into the garbage can. "I know better than that! Duh!"

"For a minute there, I thought that I over-estimated you, partner," she said. They both knew the law. Nobody goes into a pharmacy after hours. If a registered pharmacist isn't present, the doors are locked. Every pill has been inventoried, and pharmacists' licenses are on the line when pill count does not match the computer records. The law that controlled the meds, however, relegated pharmacy staff to pushing brooms and wiping down countertops.

"Somebody must have been back there during business hours, but not on the tape for the time of the robbery," said Wilson.

"That's the way that I see it, too," Megan agreed. "But those tapes are long gone. The actual thief was caught a few days later, and he was put away for awhile."

"So, where are we now? Besides at Edgewater," Darnell added.

"Do I scare you, Wilson?" She pointed her deadly eyes straight toward him.

"What do you mean?" he said to buy time.

"You're now hedging your comments. I know you're not stupid. You are the one who picked up on this crime, and I happen to think you are right. Wouldn't be here if I didn't agree."

A war of ideas broke out in Darnell's frontal cortex. "I'm not a complicated person," he began. "I think I saw something, so I reported it to my supervisors. They didn't laugh at me, but they know that if I'm right, there will be a corpse in the trunk of a car in this parking lot on September 10th. I don't think there's actually very much I can do to stop it. On the other hand, there will be a surveillance tape of this lot and we'll watch every car and truck driving into the park. We'll catch a sicko, and solve a short string of crimes. The Plain Dealer will do a write-up and I'll have a notation made in my personnel file, but…"

"But there will be a middle-aged woman dead."

"Sucks to be her!" said Darnell. Megan nodded. "But the crime will take place somewhere else, not here. I just wish..."

"Me, too," Sorento added. "You've got me hooked. When Boyd called and told me about this, he knew that I'd jump at a chance to do something, no matter how slim the odds."

"There you go," protested Wilson, "You call my commander by his first name. I don't do that, at least not to his face. You're with the FBI and I'm a ghetto kid that grew up knowing a few people who cared at the right time."

"I do scare you, then. I didn't mean to. Are we done here?"

The last question caught Wilson off guard. "What do you mean?"

"We're here at Edgewater to check out the crime scene, but we both know that the crimes were not committed here. Now we're talking about something else. We are off-duty, aren't we?"

"I'm not on the clock," Darnell said.

"Drive me somewhere," Megan implored, "somewhere where we can see the water." They left Megan's car in the lot, and Darnell turned right onto the Shoreway to where it merged onto Clifton Boulevard. He was headed west. His destination was a park called Bradstreet's Landing in Rocky River.

Chapter 10

Cuyahoga General

Davis noted the name written with a magic marker on the water pitcher on the nightstand. "Mr. Zacharias?" he asked of the gray-haired old man lying in the hospital bed. "I'm Davis McGowan, the new Interim at Old First."

The man's eyes opened for a moment then rolled shut. "Doctor McGowan," he said in a raspy voice. "Sorry if I'm a bit drowsy, I just got back from surgery."

"Yes, I know. The nurse told me that you had a pin put in your hip. She also told me that I should try to wake you up."

Zacharias smiled, "They've been giving me a hard time. I don't think they want anyone to get any rest around here." Even through the grogginess the good-natured delivery of the words told Davis that Burton Zacharias was a pleasant man.

"They told me that they're going to have you up in a chair by this afternoon and on a walker by this evening."

"As long as they don't make me wash the windows!"

The banter took McGowan by surprise.

"I think you're more alert than they give you credit for," he said.

"Gotta keep'em guessing." He reached toward his left forearm where a loop in a clear tube dipped beneath a white adhesive patch.

"They have an IV in your arm," said Davis as he reached to intercept the old man's hand. "Probably not a good idea to pull it out."

Zacharias' eyes opened wider than before and captured McGowan's. "They didn't sink the ship, did they?"

Davis looked again at Zacharias' left arm and the tattoo just beneath the bandages. It was a tanker floating on a distressed sea and the words *Booker T.* arched above like a rainbow."

"She's still afloat," answered McGowan.

"Damn straight," said Burton with a defiance that caught McGowan off guard. "Not on my watch!"

"Navy?"

"Merchant Marine," corrected Zacharias. "We were the targets that won the war."

Davis knew that there was a story about to erupt, but blood pressure was mounting, too. "How about we save the *Booker T.* until after the IV comes out? Sounds like you've got something important to say."

"Helen never liked to be around when I got into that 'ancient history' as she called it. Guess we won't have to worry about that."

McGowan had grown used to coming into the middle of situations without knowing the main characters. Helen might be his wife. By the way he spoke, was she dead? He supposed so. Colleen would know. If she were dead, there would have been some time when flowers were sent, visits were made, or address labels were changed. Davis would ask her later.

"Has the doctor told you how long you'll be here?"

"They want me to go into some nursing home for a while, but I'm going to fight. They're worried because I live alone, but I told them that there's a girl living upstairs who can check in on me."

"They probably want you close to rehab. More and more they use these nursing facilities for short periods of time, then you're back in your own place."

"That's what they say. My mother and Helen's mother both broke their hips and that was all she wrote. Both dead in a few weeks."

"That was probably awhile ago, wasn't it?"

"1958 and '59."

"Back then they used to put patients in bed when they broke a hip and they never got out of it. They're going to have you walking tonight!"

"Well, like I said, there's a girl upstairs who does a lot to help."

The visit ended when a male nurse arrived. "Okay, Burt, time to get you up in the chair. I'll help you just in case you don't have your land-legs yet."

Obviously he's already heard about the 'Booker T.' thought McGowan. "How about a short prayer and then I'll head out," offered Davis. Burton Zacharias extended a hand to Davis and closed his eyes.

After a few words, Zacharias was squeezing Davis' hand and gave a low-volume "Thank you."

He's running scared, thought McGowan. "I'll stop back tomorrow," he said. "I'll be expecting a walking tour!"

"Aye, aye," came the answer and the nurse was untangling the IV tubes and pushing them to one side to clear the edge of the bed. "Give my love to Colleen," he added.

"I will," said Davis. As he turned to leave, a familiar someone entered the room. It was Katherine Shafer.

"Now you're treading on my turf," she said, extending a hand to McGowan. She was dressed as she had been the day she covered the phones for McQuisten's surprise party. This time, however, she was accessorized with a silver and black stethoscope draped over her shoulders. "I see you've caught up with Burt, my favorite merchant marine." She threw a quick look into the room where the grimace on Zacharias' face announced that the first attempt at sitting up would be short and not sweet. The two stepped out into the corridor where their conversation could be private.

"How's he doing?" asked Davis.

"He'll be sore for awhile," she said, "but he'd teach us plenty about toughness. At sixteen he used a fire axe to knock the ice off the decks of a Liberty Boat in the North Atlantic."

"Let me guess, the *Booker T.*"

"You've heard, then?"

"Not yet, but I have a feeling I'll hear about it soon."

"He's good at telling, and it's worth hearing. We see a little old man, but there was a time when he pulled half a dozen half-burned, oil-soaked men out of freezing water."

"Sounds like I have a story coming."

"Oh, he won't tell you about that. He'll talk about his ship and his Captain. Doesn't say much about himself. I heard that from some of the scarred men that have shown up in church with him over the years. They seek him out, one by one, to show him pictures of their grandchildren."

Davis looked back through the door at the frail man fighting to sit up straight against the red vinyl upholstered chair back. Any sign of pain had been replaced by determination. "You're right, he'll be fine!" offered McGowan. "Thanks, again, for answering the phones the other day. Colleen couldn't believe that 'Dr. Shafer' was answering phones so she could go to lunch."

Katherine Shafer laughed. "Of course she couldn't! She always puts herself at the bottom of the list. I was glad to do it." Her demeanor changed, and she stepped closer and lowered her voice. "Davis, can I rely on your professional confidentiality?"

The shift caught McGowan off guard. "Of course."

"My reputation about being a hard-nosed, no-nonsense physician has been largely exaggerated. Colleen is one of those people who trembles at my approach. I've tried to set her straight, but she's all 'Yes, Dr. Shafer! Thank you, Dr. Shafer!' Burt, on the other hand…"

"Is a salty mariner," interrupted McGowan.

"Exactly! He doesn't make me nervous, but he's not a bit scared of me either."

"I'll remember that," added Davis. "In the meantime, just what did you do to get to be so fearsome?"

"Got born female," said Shafer. "You probably didn't notice, but I've been afflicted all my life, even before medical school."

"Actually, I had." Davis noted, "But professional ethics have prevented me from commenting one way or another."

The two matched grins, and then Katherine continued. "That's because we're of the same generation. I'm sixty-five, and forty years ago residency didn't look anything like *Grey's Anatomy* on television. For one thing, we weren't adolescents with arrested emotional development, and mostly, we were men!"

"So you had to jump higher and reach farther."

"Well, that's the public face of it. Actually, I just had to not play their games. We had the same credentials so I just had to out snoot them when they got huffy."

"They made you pay."

"Looking back, it wasn't so bad. Even entertaining at times. Most of the old guys are gone, and they really did become colleagues in time. Anyway, I didn't mean to tell war stories. I just wanted you to know that I respect what goes on at Old First, and I think you do as well. If you hear rumors that I'm an 'unapproachable little Hitler,' well, it's probably only half-true. Let me know if there's anything I can do to help."

"Thank you, Dr. Shafer!" said McGowan with a bowing motion.

"It's Katie, and I can throw a punch!" she answered.

"I'll bet you can," he agreed. "Thanks, Katie, I'll remember that. Take care of Burt. He has some stories that I want to hear."

Chapter 11

Bradstreet's Landing

When Darnell turned in at the park entrance, Megan became aware of their destination. "I'd almost forgotten about this place," she remarked. Wilson pulled his black Impala into a space in the sparsely populated lot. They had driven across Lakewood and were now near the western edge of Rocky River.

"I think Westsiders are more oriented to the Lake than those who live in the Heights." His comment could have set off a long-time Cleveland debate between east and west, but Megan didn't bite.

"You may be right," she said. "To me the heart of the city has always been University Circle. It is different out here, flatter and more open."

"I grew up on the East Side," offered Darnell, "some of my teachers lived in Shaker, but I was closer to home at the bottom of Cedar Hill." His comment was not about geography, but a socio-economic gap that he knew could loom between himself and his, dare he think it, "partner."

Again, Sorento did not take the bait or ask for clarification. To her it seemed a given that was far less consequential than the thoughts that now carried her. She had asked for this excursion. She had asked for this time and place, though not by name. On the lake and off the record were her prerequisites and Bradstreet's Landing, with its long break wall extending offshore was perfect.

"Let's take a walk," she said. They stepped out of the car and moved toward the pier. The breeze was onshore and cool in the August sun, the sky clear enough to see the watery horizon. The sailboats were still playing the wind, but it was impossible to tell if either of these was one they had seen from East Lakeside Drive.

"You asked me how I knew Boyd Wakeman. Well, the answer is a little personal, but I thought that you deserved some kind of explanation, being that he's your boss and all."

Darnell's mind raced ahead. He had not anticipated the word "personal". Maybe a family friend, but that would hardly need a change of venue to tell. If they were lovers, he'd be guilty of two counts of bad character judgment. He did what good detectives do best; he listened and watched.

By now, they were approaching the sandy strand that formed the shoreline east and west. To the right, the glass features of city skyline gleamed in the reflected sunlight. "Cleveland gets a bad rap, doesn't it?" she observed. Wilson stepped up beside her to share her perspective.

"It's the only place I really know," he confessed, "so it seems like home. When the Indians, Browns, or Cavs are winning, people seem to love the city. The rest of the time... well, most of the people just whine a lot about the weather."

"Not much to complain about today!"

"Actually, most days. I think people just enjoy the sport of running down the place. I had a teacher, Ms. Brown. She'd bawl me out if I ever whined about my life. She'd say, 'Darnell Wilson, do you want to do something or just feel sorry for yourself? I don't go wasting my time on pity!'"

"She sounds tough."

"Not really. She just didn't allow any 'negative self-talk.' That's the way she'd put it. I owe her a lot."

"Well, I'll try not to whine. Ms. Brown's rules apply. If I start to pity myself, you have my permission to call me out. Okay?"

"Sure." Wilson wasn't fully aware of what he had agreed to, but he went along.

Megan took a deep breath. "My brother was killed when I was still in high school. We were always close growing up. When he went off to college at Akron, we'd talk on the phone a couple of times a week. My Dad got tired of the phone bills at home, so he bought me a cell phone–even before they became popular. Anyway, he was supposed to come home one weekend. This was in his junior year. He called me on a Friday night to say he'd be home by lunch on Saturday. He was going out with some friends. Anyway, he wasn't home by noon, and his phone must have been turned off because it just kept going to voice mail.

"I called his roommates and they had no clue. They thought he had come home the night before. Obviously, whoever he went out with were not normal friends. The Akron police weren't racing to find out what happened to him. An Akron U. guy goes out drinking on Friday night and doesn't come home the next day… not a high priority, but they took a report. A week later, they went to campus and talked to the guys he shared an apartment with. They were still clueless. From the University's perspective, this was all off-campus and outside their jurisdiction.

"We were all going crazy, and it seemed like we were the only ones. My friends and I copied fliers and posted them all around campus. My Dad wanted to get the news media to pay attention, but it was just a footnote on the morning news. Then he got a call from your boss. Boyd had heard the report and called Channel Three. They gave him our number."

"But wasn't he already in Lakewood back then?"

"That's right. The first thing he did was explain that this was not his business. He wasn't calling as a cop; he was calling as a father."

"What the hell?" Darnell wanted to pull the words back into his mouth.

"Exactly," said Megan without missing a beat. "He had no business, but… well, I think a lot of your Boyd Wakeman. He's a real man in a world of phonies. He gave us a few contacts and made a few calls himself. People started to pay attention."

"Did they find him? Your brother, I mean."

Megan turned to look toward the horizon or to a distant sailboat. The light that had been reflecting from the glass towers now caught a tear on her cheek. Without thinking, Darnell gently brushed it away with his right forefinger.

"Ms. Brown would be giving me a lecture now, wouldn't she?" said Sorento.

"I don't think so," said Wilson.

They were moving slowly along the walkway, a paved break wall of massive limestone blocks. A few people in lawn chairs with bait buckets alongside were fishing at the far end of the jetty. The lake was not particularly rough, but occasional wake from a passing powerboat would send some spray flying onto the black stones. A chain-link fence ran along the edge of the walkway to keep people off the rocks. Darnell turned to lean against the rail. He looked at Sorento, but she was still looking at something far away.

"Ms. Brown knew the difference between self-pity and tears. He was your brother."

"They found him along a back road in Huron County."

"Huron County?"

"He was tied to a fencepost with his underwear stuffed in his mouth."

Wilson could almost guess the rest. "Was your brother a homosexual?"

"No! Yes! I don't know. We had talked once about it. Well, I mostly listened. He liked girls, but he found this video on the Internet of two guys. Well he just said that he was aroused by it. He thought that it should have turned him off, but...

"Anyway, it was pretty clear that it was a hate crime. We guess that he went to a Gay bar somewhere, probably not in Akron. Somebody there targeted him or a couple of people saw him coming out and picked him up."

"Who's 'we?' You and your father?"

"No, my Dad never could accept that. His son was straight and he knew it. Boyd was really gentle with him, never pushed. I was the one who talked to the official investigators."

"The FBI," said Darnell.

"It was ruled a hate crime and they were brought in. I needed to understand how people could think like that. How they could hate somebody dead, somebody they didn't even know, somebody's son."

"Somebody's brother," added Wilson. Megan turned to him with liquid brown eyes and a sadness that could not be masked. He had nothing to say, so he opened his arms and she slipped into his compassion.

"Ms. Brown would have been proud of you. 'Megan Sorento,' she'd say, 'you did something.'"

"I hope so. Didn't do much for my brother. But you're right. That's why I try profiling, that's why Boyd Wakeman knew that I'd help you, and that's why I call him by his first name. He's not a cop to my family; he helped us bring my brother home."

"If it's any help, I've always respected him, but for different reasons." Suddenly Darnell became aware of his arms and the hug was over. Megan used her palms to smudge away the dampness from her cheeks. Her composure returned like an actor anticipating a change of scene.

"Darnell?" she asked.

"What?"

"If you ever tell anyone that I lost it when I told you this, I will rip your tongue right out of your face and use it to clean the toilet."

"Damn!" he said, "I could have sworn that Megan was just here. Did you see her leave, Agent Sorento?" They both laughed.

"Well, you did see her, but I have to warn you, she doesn't get out very often," said Megan.

"I was going to ask her if she'd like to get something to eat, maybe a drink," said Darnell. "Since she's gone, maybe you'd like to join me."

"So you'll ask me on the rebound, but I'm not your first choice."

"A very close second. Besides, you're my partner."

"That's true," said Sorento. "Just promise you won't keep looking around for Megan."

"I promise." The two walked back toward the car. "Where do you want to eat?" asked Darnell.

Chapter 12

The Western Reserve

"You've never had this long a commute before," said Beth, "and I feel like you are now orbiting in another universe."

"I am, I suppose. But, it's only temporary. Their search committee is up and running and I think they'll be ready to call a new pastor by spring."

Beth laughed. "You need to start sitting in the back row on Sunday morning. There's a posse gathering members to tell the committee to slow down and take their time. It seems they like the new guy!"

"Yeah, but wait until they get to know me." Now it was Davis' turn to laugh.

"We have an ace in the hole, though. I keep turning that card over to remind them that my interim contract is for one year and not automatically renewable. In the meantime, there's no reason why you couldn't commute with me. I hear Cleveland is lovely this time of year." Even though he was saying the words, he couldn't help but be reminded of a period in their marriage when she fought against the idea that her identity was held captive by Davis' profession.

"Lovely now, but wait until January," said Beth.

"Bah-humbug!" barked Davis. "We can go into hibernation then anyway."

"If we did go in together one day each week, what would I be doing?"

"Church activities might work." Beth scowled. "Or there're restaurants, the Indians, the Cavs, the Playhouse, Severance Hall. I'm sure there'd be plenty of after-work venues."

"Date night has never been a problem, but what do I do while you're at the hospitals or in the office?"

McGowan thought twice about suggesting the stereotypical tagalong role of the minister's wife. "The library is within walking distance from the church."

It was Beth's turn to consider. "Do you think they'd open their archives to an amateur historian?"

"I think that's their job," said Davis. "You've been wanting to write something about the two Ohios." In most of the road atlases, Ohio is divided north and south by I-70. The fact is that McNally got it right. Northern Ohio was settled out of Massachusetts and Connecticut. Southern Ohio out of Virginia and Kentucky with the Mason-Dixon Line running along the parallel of Patterson Road in Dayton.

"I must be getting old," she confessed. Davis almost got whiplash at the sudden turn in the conversation.

"Did I miss something?"

"No, I just had a sort of revelation. You named all those adventurous ideas and I really like the idea of getting lost in research about the founding of the Western Reserve."

"Well, if you've gotten old, then we've managed to do it together."

"I said 'getting' not 'gotten'," corrected Beth with a smile that betrayed her.

"Sorry," said Davis with mock apology. "I meant to say that it must be frustrating for somebody who's still 'getting' to be married to an old man."

"If you only knew," said Beth as she slid an arm around him and pulled him close for a kiss. "Promise me, then that you won't tell him. There's really no reason he should know about us. Don't know if his heart could take it. Promise?"

"It's our secret."

"What do you say to meeting on the sly in Cleveland?"

"Discretion is the key. I won't tell your husband, if you don't tell my wife."

"I think it's going to be kinda nice to have something going on with a younger man!"

"You mean, instead of that retired guy you've been living with?" said Davis.

Chapter 13

First Date

In retirement, Davis had nearly forgotten about the realities of parish life. In his mind the day was laid out in neatly arranged blocks of time. It had, however, taken unexpected turns from his arrival in the office at 9:00. It began when Jenks Jenkens reported that the church had failed its annual elevator inspection. Nothing had changed in the mechanics or the equipment. What had changed was the city's inspector. Jenks, who took pride in the building's appearance and integrity, was taking the whole thing personally.

"This new fellow," he began, "has decided that we are in violation of some law because the wire that triggers the door release latch on Ontario passes through the elevator shaft."

"Is he right?" asked McGowan.

"Well, yes, but it's been that way for fourteen years and we ain't never had no inspector complain about any compliance."

"Maybe the codes have been changed?"

"No, he says that it's been that way forever and that the previous inspector was too damn lazy to write us up. That's exactly what he said 'too damn lazy'. Not my words, Reverend."

"What are our options? Did he make any suggestions?"

"Him? No suggestions, just threats. Hands me a card with his title and cell phone and says to call when we get it fixed. Until then, he says that the wire means we can't use the elevator, and without the elevator, we aren't a handicapped accessible building and he'll shut us down."

"Jenks, I think you might have encountered one of the most powerful beings in the universe. You're lucky to have escaped with your life!"

Jenks turned a confused face toward Davis and met a broad smile. In an instant, he caught the joke.

"Yes, Sir, I suppose I did," he played along.

"So all we really need to do is reroute a wire out of the elevator shaft."

"A low voltage wire," added Jenkens. "The people who installed the security latch on the door said that was the easiest way to pass the wire up from the electrical room where the connections are made."

"Jenks, how comfortable are you with moving the wire? Either we find another path up from the basement or put it inside a conduit. Could you do either of those things?"

"I was here when the door guys put it in. They looked everywhere and said they'd need a jackhammer to get through the concrete."

"Okay," said Davis. "Let me have his number. I'm going to approach the almighty with groveling repentance and see if we can get an agreement. If that doesn't work, I'm sure that there is someone in the City Engineer's office that will have a solution."

At this Jenks laughed. "You mean someone who knows how to squash a bug?"

"Now you are putting words in my mouth. If there's really something dangerous here, we'll fix it. If it's the new guy flexing his muscle, well..."

That was how the day began. The call to the inspector lasted twenty-five minutes with Davis apologizing for sins of omission, commission, and the Spanish Inquisition. In the end, it was agreed that placing the wire within a metal conduit would work and that two weeks would be a reasonable time frame.

It was nearly three o'clock before he walked in on Burt Zacharias in his hospital room. This time he could not escape his tour of the *Booker T. Washington*, a World War II Liberty Ship.

"I grew up in San Diego," said Zacharias. "I was only sixteen when the news came about Pearl Harbor. I had nothing going for me at home. I was tired of dragging my father home from the bars in the morning only to have him beat the crap out of me. It was his way of saying, 'thanks,' I guess. I had grown up on boats but the Navy recruiter didn't buy that I was eighteen, and a lot of people who were the right age were flooding the station anyway.

"I knew plenty of longshoremen. My dad had worked the docks before he fell into a bottle. Everybody heard on the radio about Roosevelt's Lend-Lease program, but the guys on the dock also knew that a thousand ships had been sunk by U-boats the year before. Lost ships meant lost crews. So, I figured they needed mariners and wouldn't be so quick to call my bluff when I told him that I just had a baby face.

"Course, it was just luck that landed me on the *Booker T.* under the best damn Captain in the war, military or civilian."

"And who was that?" asked Davis.

Burt smiled as if to say, *You really didn't need to ask; I was going to tell you regardless!* "Captain Hugh Mulzac," he said. "Twenty-two round trips across the Atlantic in five years. Kept his boat under him for all that time. Took care of his men and we were a ragtag bunch. Eighteen nationalities! Hell, we were a floating United Nations before that group ever met."

"And he kept everyone together?" said McGowan.

"Some officers are tough on the outside, walk around like hard-asses threatening everyone with the bars on their sleeves. Our Captain was tough on the inside. Had his captain's license since the first big war, but he was a black man and some of the small-minded brass weren't sure a *Negro* could command a ship–some had other names they used, but they're fighting words to me! He was a *man*, and those that served beneath him all wear the *Booker T.* under our skin." Then he added, "Or on it," looking at the tattoo on his forearm.

"Sounds like quite a man."

"He was! Took us across and back twenty-two times. We carried every kind of cargo, eighteen thousand soldiers. Most of them were throwing up in the bilges while us monkeys were knocking the ice off the railings. The regular Navy hated us, but we had better efficiency than they did."

"Professional jealousy?" asked Davis.

"No. Worse. Navy wanted to take us over. We weren't 'military' enough for their liking. We had some kids come over from the Navy. Been through a basic training and they were called able seamen, but there was nothing able about them. Navy taught them to march in rows and keep their caps square on their heads. We had to teach them about the heart and guts of a living ship. They learned, some faster than others.

"Forget what you've heard about the Merchant Marine. We were civilian patriots. Did the country's dangerous work for a fair wage and no GI Bill."

"I've got to confess that what you're telling me is the most I've ever heard of the Merchant Marine," said McGowan. Zacharias went silent and turned liquid eyes toward the maze of air handlers and vents on the graveled roof.

"It's a long story, best told with a shot and a beer, Reverend. Not sure that my stomach or your ears can handle it."

"I'll bet you'd be surprised," offered McGowan, "on both counts. You never struck me as a wimp." His tone of voice brought Burt back into the room.

"Okay," he said. "When I get home, we can pull out something cold and I'll confess all my Communist connections."

The last comment confused Davis, but he postponed a follow-up. Instead, he asked the medical option, "Are they going to discharge you directly to home?"

"I don't give a damn where they discharge me to; I know where I'm going. Doc Shafer knows me well enough to not try that."

The strength of the comment stopped the conversation, and McGowan knew it was true. "I'll see you at home then," he said.

"If I can't answer the door, Colleen can tell you where we hide the key."

"Colleen?" asked Davis.

"Colleen McQuisten. Your secretary. She lives upstairs."

"Oh," said Davis, "you mentioned once that 'a girl lived upstairs,' but I never put it together. She shares your duplex, then?"

"It's a *double*; there are no *duplexes* in Lakewood," quipped Zacharias with a wink. "It's a local thing," he added. "She's lived up there thirty-eight years. Her son and my son are best friends. Grew up like brothers."

"Shows how little I know about Colleen. Didn't know she had children."

"Doc, we don't have children anymore; we have adults. Hugh and Bobby are middle-aged men with families of their own."

"Okay, which is which?"

"Bobby is Colleen's named after his father who was 'Robert Jerome'. We called her husband 'Jerry' though, and I suppose I should call Bobby 'Robert' since he's grown. He's in advertising now, in Chicago. He has a pretty wife, two kids, and the American Dream. His mother did things right, in spite of everything else."

McGowan knew that there was a larger story, but he didn't need to hear it unless it were offered freely.

"Hugh is our boy. Made Helen and me very proud." Davis could hear a slight faltering at the naming of his wife. "Mechanical engineer. Went to Case, here in Cleveland before it joined with Western Reserve; that was a while ago." Davis understood. When he was a boy, the Case Institute of Technology was part of Cleveland's institutional vocabulary. "'Hugh Mulzac Zacharias.' I always told him it was a big name to live up to, but he did."

McGowan had heard the first two parts of that name before and his brain rushed to recall. "He was the captain of the *Booker T. Washington*, wasn't he?" The fact didn't actually strike his consciousness until he heard the name in his own voice.

Burt smiled. "McGowan, I'll take on anyone who tries to tell me that you don't pay attention. Most young people today don't listen, much less remember, the rantings of an old man. But you got the captain and the ship."

Davis laughed. "I have not been called 'young' for a long time!" he quipped.

"It's that Einstein thing," said Zacharias, "it's all relative. I'm eighty-seven and what are you, fifty-five?"

"You're nearly a decade off," retorted Davis.

"I know," Burt confessed, "I may be old, but I do understand politics." In that moment the two men crossed a line that divided the personal and professional. They had become friends. It happened so quickly that McGowan had not seen it coming. That's the way it seemed to be with male friendships. They came in moments of work or banter when all rivalry and self-interest were completely abandoned.

This was a lesson that had been reinforced over and over, especially by the veterans of World War II. "There are no atheists in foxholes" was the cliché that would be spoken, but that truism was invariably followed by a pause. Davis could guess the images that exploded in the memory of the speakers. They were like the photos that went into the TV documentaries, but more personal. The thought images carried names of men whose self-interest vaporized in the flash of fire, and they only thought to keep a brother alive. Burt had been in the Merchant Marine, and Davis suspected that he had seen such faces under fire.

"So you are going to push being discharged to your house?" he said in an attempt to bring the discussion back to the correct time zone.

"One thing I've learned," began Burt, "is that these doctors can fume and fuss, but they can't really order you around unless you let them."

"I suppose, that's so," said Davis hesitatingly. "They could always say that your insurance wouldn't allow it."

Zacharias grinned, "Ah, but they'd be lying for sure. My insurance company would rather me go home and die from lack of proper care than run up a month's worth of bills at a place where the food has never even gotten close to a salt shaker and the booze is measured out with a thimble."

It was McGowan's turn to grin. "Okay," he said, "I'll not try to convince you of anything. You're determined enough to beat them all at their games. Go home, and I'll catch up with you there. I can get the address from my secretary!"

"You're a smart man, Davis McGowan. You know when you're in a fight you can't win." His lighthearted expression dropped suddenly from his face. "I'll let you in on something, but I'll only tell you once. I'm eighty-seven and never thought that I would live forever. I've seen too much to believe in that fairy tale. You tell people this more than once and they say you're depressed and send in some psychologist who doesn't know their ass from their elbow. Most of the people that I've loved have already crossed, and there are times when it only seems right that I should be in their company again. I like having good people around, so you're welcome, but just don't try to fix me too much. I want my friends to recognize me when I get there. Do you understand?"

Davis nodded. "Maybe even more than you'd expect. I'll make you a deal. We'll keep company and watch each other's backs. I'd be a fool to not want you on my side."

"Deal."

* * * *

When Davis returned from Cuyahoga General, he was already late for his appointed date with Beth. She had spent the day at the library, but it was nearly 5:30. Colleen had left before five to catch her bus and Beth was waiting in Davis' office. "Sorry," he said as he gave her a quick kiss.

"It's been a good day, so you're forgiven. Actually this building would be a spooky place if everyone were gone."

"You mean they aren't?" asked Davis.

"No, the staff here works your hours! Alistair Montgomery is helping a couple who are picking music for their wedding and Bob Craig is meeting with them afterward for premarital counseling. Jenks is around here, too. I think he's an unofficial security agent. He sticks his head in now and again to see that I'm alright."

As if on cue, Jenks Jenkens passed by the open door. "Boss is here," he said, "better look busy." The comment was followed with a hearty laugh and the arrival of the utility cart he was pulling along behind with its assortment of brooms, spray bottles, and garbage bags. "I get so tired of cleaning up the messes these Presbyterians leave behind."

"Me, too!" shouted McGowan in response. "Then again, it keeps us employed!"

"Got that right," and the cart lumbered around the corner.

"Well, my Dear, I think Mr. Jenkens has everything under control, why don't we head out for dinner?"

"Have a place in mind?" asked Beth.

"How about seafood?" suggested Davis, "I heard about this little place down the street!"

Chapter 14

Just Off Clifton

Rachael rarely disappointed him. Tonight she was right on time. She got off the No. 55 bus on the south side of Clifton Boulevard at 4:53 p.m. and walked west to the corner and then south.

Kosten waited in his van until she turned out of sight. He twisted the ignition until the engine squealed to life, slipped the gear selector into drive, and pulled away from the curb. He already knew where she lived; he'd been in front of her house before. He just wanted to be sure that she would be faithful to her routine. After all, it was Wednesday; she would come home, drop off her current book for reading on the bus, and go out to the garage. It was her evening to make a quick run to the grocery. She would return in a half an hour with three or four recycle bags of groceries and a clear-domed container heaped with salad for a dinner.

It did not strike Richard as being odd that a woman with her own car would ride the bus each day. Downtown parking was not cheap and the foregoing of all the winter-salted commuter miles kept her 1998 metallic-blue Buick Skylark from showing its true age.

He wedged the van between two cars and waited in plain sight of the driveway which ran along the left side of the two-and-a-half story house and back to the diminutive garage. He guessed the house was built in the twenties or thirties and the garage added later, maybe in the 1950s when most people could not imagine needing more than one stall to house their car.

Before ten minutes passed, the small overhead door began to lift and Richard could see that it was a tight fit between the side-view mirrors and the doorframe. There was not much space in the garage itself. Still the view was fairly sheltered by the house on one side and the overgrown row of arborvitae along the adjacent property line. He would park his van on the apron of the drive, and there would be plenty of room for what needed to be done. It would just be a matter of popping the trunk on the Skylark. With any luck, there'd be a release button on the key ring, and Rachael would be resting quietly inside when he went back to move the van and get on his scrubs.

The blue car backed toward the street, stopped at the curb, then inched out to the south toward Detroit Avenue and the shopping district. Kosten looked aside at an imaginary clipboard in case she looked toward the non-descript white van. He then sat for five minutes. He always watched the clock. A minute can seem like five if adrenalin is flowing. Clocks are safer against a too soon return by a forgetful Rachael. But she did not forget anything.

He would have liked a cigarette, but Rachael didn't smoke and some people have enough sensitivity to detect a recent presence. He got out of the van and walked to her front door. He rang the bell. No sounds came from inside, not even a foo-foo dog. He rang the bell again, this time putting an ear closer to the door to make sure that it sounded within the house. The chime was clear and distinct, just as he expected, just as he hoped. He thought about walking around back, but this was a nice quiet residential street, the perfect breeding ground for nosy neighbors who would be all too anxious to report a young man in a non-descript white panel van.

He had been thinking about ligatures and was leaning toward a forty-eight inch zip tie, the mammoth cousin of the little ones that frustrated all sorts of packaging. They always had to be cut with scissors or knives to free computer cords from their cardboard backing. He also liked the sound when they were zipped tight, and the relentless grip that they offered. Most were too small, however, for his purpose, only a few inches. Richard was impressed when he saw a large one at an area home center. Forty-eight inches for a bundle of massive cables or one neck. It would loop easily over the head, then, zip. There would be no struggle, except against the unyielding nylon that would not give before red turned to blue and his mother would not complain about him anymore.

Kosten did not want to be seen buying a package, so he kept an eye out for bundled wire. The stores he cleaned were full of cables that connected registers and lights and satellite hookups. Electricians were trained to keep their bundled wire neat, straight, and well-anchored. Releasing one with the sharp point of his lock-back knife was easy. Weeks went by and no one seemed to notice, or at least they did not feel that any replacement was necessary.

It was these small victories that gave him confidence. Richard had read enough detective stories to know that investigators would go to the suspect's house to find matching duct tape and plastic bags or to surveillance tapes of people buying similar products at local stores. He felt some triumph in thinking this through so clearly. Who could they accuse with a commercial grade zip tie from an electrical contractor?

As he thought it, the nylon tie was sitting coiled in a peanut butter jar filled with isopropyl alcohol. He would not touch it again without latex gloves. Not gloves he ever purchased, and not the gloves issued by his employer. These had been recovered from the trash after a busy day at the pharmacy when they had given sixty-two seasonal flu shots. No one would ever find the gloves, but if they did, the DNA would be a jigsaw puzzle.

It was dinner time. Rachael had gone over to shop on Detroit. He would go, too, not for groceries, but to grab a grilled cheese sandwich at a local hot spot. If that was too busy, Panera Bread was across the street and they had good black bean soup and a cute waitress who was not averse to flirting.

Chapter 15

The Blue Point Grille

Davis had promised seafood, and the Blue Point would not disappoint his wife on their first Wednesday date night in Cleveland. It was still early in the evening when they arrived, and that perhaps explained the fact that there were so many open tables. Cleveland's night life was slow in the midweek and when the sports venues were idle. The city of the Indians, Browns, and Cavaliers continued to have hope, not only for the future of its sports, but also for the renaissance of its soul. The current hope was called Med Mart, a commercial venture for medical providers based on the city's long history of medical innovation and practice and care. The second hope, 'more dicey' in McGowan's telling, was the legalization of casino gambling. It was a pun he often used, but it spoke to his early career experience. While at Princeton in the '70s, he saw firsthand the façade of glitz that covered the nearby poverty of Atlantic City. Still, there was hope in this once great city of gritty industry and commerce.

There was only one other couple seated in the vicinity of the McGowan's table. They might have been half Davis' and Beth's age. Davis was buried in the menu when Beth was first to speak.

"Business or pleasure?"

"What?" said a confused Davis looking up from the menu.

"Those two," she said, indicating the young people. They were dressed casually as if they had come from an afternoon out of doors. He was slim and athletic with the features of an African-American model. She was petite, dark-haired with deep-brown eyes looking out from an olive complexion. As fashion models go, she was too short and full-bodied. As women go, she was strikingly perfect.

Davis had played this guessing game before. They seemed intent in their conversation, as if discussing a problem or some theory. "Business," was his guess.

"She has been crying," offered Beth as though raising the ante on the pot.

McGowan looked again. He was the one who always pointed out body language, but he had missed this one. "You're right. But they're not sitting like this is a date."

"Maybe a first date?" said Beth.

"Crying on a first date isn't a particularly good omen, is it?"

"Maybe he's acting like the consoling older brother in order to get closer. Look at how attentive he is." Just then the man turned toward the McGowans as if he were suddenly aware of his audience. They turned back toward each other. "Do you remember when we were first dating?" asked Beth.

Davis smiled, "Of course. We wondered if people were beginning to see us as a couple, and whether we made a match. We knew it, but were almost afraid that others would guess us out. Strange time!"

"We were younger. I think we were expected to get started earlier. My, but I sound old to myself!"

"At some point, I think we got old together," said Davis. "It's not all bad, is it? I mean, growing old together." He reached across the table and took Beth's hand.

"I think that I'm supposed to spill my water glass on you and stomp off for calling me old, but you're right. I think I'd rather be us than them, just starting out, I mean."

"So you're still trying to figure them out?" They looked back toward the other table. The man had set his hand on hers and she turned liquid eyes toward his face. "He's interested," said Davis.

"She is, too," added Beth. "Women can tell these things," she added.

"No fair playing the intuition card," complained Davis.

"Think about what you just said," offered Beth. "Maybe we are the first outsiders to see them as a couple. Maybe even before they know it themselves."

"Enough about them," said Davis, "I brought you to this swanky place to try to lure you back to my place. It's supposed to have the best seafood in town from the Maine lobsters to the Lake Erie Perch."

"Your place? I notice that you are wearing a wedding band; what kind of woman do you think I am?"

"I'm hoping that you're not the kind of prude that would object to running around with a married man."

"Normally, Dr. McGowan, I would take offence at such a proposal, but since you are buying dinner, and it's you proposing to do the luring, I might be persuaded to go home with you tonight."

"Whoa, the old guy might score!" said Davis.

"Maybe," answered Beth, "but my guess is that your wife will be the one who decides that!"

"Yes, Dear!"

Chapter 16

New Patterns

Intellectually, Davis was aware that churches in urban centers functioned differently than those in the 'burbs. At Covenant Church in Dayton, his session meetings took place on Monday nights so board members could schedule business trips for the midweek and still catch the redeye home by Friday evening. A very few avoided the airline schedule by the use of a corporate jet, but with cutbacks that had become much rarer.

Here at Old First, the meetings were apt to be short and tied to the beginning or the end of the work day so that people could rush out of the city for dinner either at home or on the continuous run that was the America of fast food and instant communication. The mantras on Public Square were more commonly: "Can we meet at 4:30?," "How about before church?" "What about after services on Sunday?" With growing popularity was the more distressing "send an e-mail" or "text me when you find out."

McGowan had two internal responses to this way of doing the congregation's business. First, he felt old and missed the days when sending a message via windows meant leaning out of the second story to razz a neighbor about washing his car too often and causing the current bout of rain. Second, he worried about the disconnections that were running rampant. From his ancient perspective, the head of any religious organization is a person who believes in community. Churches, synagogues, and mosques are places where values are vocalized and, hopefully, set into positive motion both within the circle of believers and the neighborhood of a larger world. All the meeting shortcuts seemed like time bombs for a fight. There was just too little awareness of the importance of the meeting-after-the-meeting.

It seemed like a casualty of the sexual revolution. Somehow, in the struggle for gender equality, the meeting-after-the-meeting became an evil vestige of the 'old boy' network. It was characterized as taking place in the proverbial smoke-filled room with a saccharine condescension about women not enduring secondhand smoke. Sometimes it was described as taking place on golf courses or along a row of urinals in the locker room at the club.

In his early years in ministry, Davis recalled that the only agenda at such meetings was a pizza and catching up on regional jokes. Women and men sat around such tables, and business was never the issue. It was about play. Not playing in the sense of "around," but in the sense of childhood friends whose trust survives the corruption of adulthood. McGowan knew that strong congregations have, somewhere along the way, learned to play well together. "There is more trust in childhood play than in a notarized contract," he would say to younger ministers who were looking at him blankly. Again, he was feeling old. They understood play. They had an app for that!

Still, Davis struggled to learn this urban, meeting-around-the-edges culture. Yes, he could meet before church this Sunday at 8:00 a.m. Yes, it would mean leaving Huron at 7:00. Yes, the session did need to increase the administrative line item for more members of the pastoral search committee to fly to Seattle to meet with someone who looked really good on paper. No, he did not agree that a teleconference could accomplish the same thing. Yes, a multinational can run on technology; they also have legal departments. Of course you'll want to find a new pastor who's up-to-date on all the new technologies. No offence taken, I use technology when it suits me. It doesn't always suit me. A few years ago I was a Young Turk, now I'm just an Old Fart.

"Thank God, you're *our* Old Fart," came the friendly voice of Fred Reynolds.

"So the motion is to increase the budget of the search committee by $5,000. The budget is to be balanced by reducing the line item for the Interim Pastor which will be under-spent because I did not come on board until four weeks ago and the position was vacant for June and July. All in favor... All opposed... The motion is passed." (*And, that,* thought McGowan, *is a victory for Old Farts and community.*)

"You know, eight o'clock on a Sunday morning is not very user friendly," noted Martin Humphries as the meeting broke up.

McGowan could feel tension rising. Since retiring, he noticed his tolerance toward a naysayer was just about gone. He was tempted to say, "Tell me about it, my drive here was an hour longer than yours," but he knew his cynicism would be wasted. Instead, he pulled back to a tighter line of political correctness. "I'm sorry. It's inconvenient for me, too, but I need to keep the time following the service to talk with visitors or people who feel a sudden need to speak with a pastor."

The fact was that his more likely task would be to make sure that the office area was securely locked. This, too, was a hold-over from previous congregations, which were not as security conscious as Old First had to be. Humphries' reaction told him that his after-church activity would be monitored, so he was glad when, following the after-service surge for the door, a young couple remained behind. His first thought was that here was a couple church shopping for the right venue to be the backdrop of a wedding. As an interim pastor, McGowan was reluctant to schedule anything too far into the future. From the point of view of his contract, he was to be replaced soon, and his role was to provide temporary continuity for a community that had begun in 1820 and would extend beyond Davis' ability to drive the necessary commuter miles.

His first impression, however, ended with the glint of a gold band on the young man's left hand. There was something else, the familiarity of man and boy. He spoke before his brain had time to analyze the word. "Matt?"

The man's face broke into a smile. He was remembered. It was more this reaction than the naming that flooded McGowan's memory. This was Matt Fornesby, but he had been a sixteen-year-old in Dayton, Ohio when they last spoke.

"Last I knew of you, Matt, you were a student at Northwestern."

"That was a while ago, Dr. McGowan. I graduated six years ago. After that I moved to Indianapolis for work, and met someone special."

He turned to the young brunette at his side. "This is Erin Speer, my wife. She's why I'm here today."

"So, I have you to thank," said McGowan. "You must have power if you can deliver such a blast from the past."

"Actually," said Erin in a firm voice, "it's less impressive, I have a job interview here in Cleveland and Matt insisted that we schedule over a Sunday to see you."

Davis could still see in Matt the face of the sixteen-year-old that he had awakened to tell that his mother had just died in her bedroom down the hall. On that early morning, Matt's father, Barker, had lost his wife to complications of her diabetes and faced a cascading series of events. He had called McGowan with the news, and Davis stood with him through the night of disbelief.

"How's your father?" asked McGowan.

"He's fine. He's the one who knew that you were preaching again here in Cleveland." McGowan wondered at the fact that Barker would have paid any attention after all the years. Davis had seen his name in *Time* and

The Wall Street Journal when commentators were agog at Barker Fornesby's use of a poison pill to avert a hostile takeover. Less than a year later, the game was reversed and he took over the same competitor in a move that caught them in freefall from their over-extended balance sheet. Suddenly his mind was flooded with questions, some of which were born of the years between and some from the secrets that Davis was sworn to keep.

"What is your schedule like?" asked Davis. "Can we take you and Erin out for coffee or brunch? Or do you want to look for fossils?"

Matt's wry smile toward Erin told McGowan that he had just won Matt a bet or something.

"We're free for the day. That would be great; Erin's interviews don't begin until early tomorrow."

"Where are you interviewing?"

"At University Circle Hospital. I'm a physician," she added, "I'm looking into a position they have open there."

"She's one of the finalists," bragged Matt, "they've been recruiting like it's Ohio State football."

"Not Northwestern?" bantered McGowan.

"Don't get him started," warned Erin.

"Okay," answered Davis, "we're too close to the season and you guys are currently from the Hoosier State. Does Ohio feel safe to you?"

All three laughed in unison as Beth walked up to where they stood in the vestibule. She immediately recognized the young man. "Matt?"

"Mrs. McGowan," he responded.

"Have I aged that much?" she added with the flicker of recollection.

"Beth, this is Erin Speer, Matt's wife," offered Davis with an emphasis on the final word.

"This is wonderful," she responded, "are you here for very long?"

"I've already invited them to brunch; the only thing left to decide is where. John Q doesn't open until 4:00 on Sunday. There's the food court at Tower City across the Square, not very fancy."

"We're staying at the Renaissance Hotel. They have a few nice restaurants," declared Matt.

"Sounds good," said Davis. "Let me ditch my robe and we'll head out." With that he turned back toward the office and the Ontario Street lobby. In the corner of his peripheral vision he could see Beth and the other two following slowly. They would be at the door by the time he dropped off his clerical robe and hood, his standard Sunday uniform. In his hurry, he did notice Martin Humphries standing near the visitors' desk. "New physician being recruited by University Circle Hospital," he said as an aside as he rushed past. "I'm taking them to brunch. Thought it would be a good way to get the old foot in the door."

Humphries eyes bounced open wide. "Good idea," he said. Inside Davis was savoring an almost sinful sense of triumph. It was not the half-truth that he had just touted, but the reality that he had just played to Martin's weakness. Every congregation had this type, the people who played to privilege and bowed to status. It was not that their motives were flawed. They just didn't always see common humanity as a more compelling force than institutional market-share. If Matt were anything like his high-powered father, he would know the difference. Davis was comfortable in his assumption that Matt would see the clear distinction between the ideas of mission and marketing.

* * * *

In spite of the fact that it was only 11:30, it was hot air radiating off the sidewalk that met them when they opened the door on Ontario. A woman was walking past moving toward Public Square. Davis recognized her from Colleen's anniversary party.

"Rachael?"

"Oh, hi, Dr. McGowan."

"Are you on your way to work? Is the restaurant open now?"

"No, we're not open, at least not normally. We have a private party in there for lunch, so I'm going to help set up and serve."

"I know this would be cheating, but have you ever thought of having your friend, Colleen, validate your parking pass and you could park in our lot for free?"

"Dr. McGowan!" she said with mock incredulity. "I am shocked. Besides, with my luck I'd get ratted out and both Colleen and I would get in trouble. I don't mess with her, she's my lifeline. She just dropped me off, in fact. No buses on Sunday anymore, but she said she was on her way to see Mr. Zacharias at the hospital, so she just went a little out of the way."

"Well, good luck with your lunch party. Would have been nice if you'd been open. We have friends in from out of town," said Davis, nodding toward the young couple.

"Thanks, Dr. McGowan. Have a good visit." With that, she was back on her path. Davis wondered how she planned to get back home. It was none of his business, but it reminded him of the concerns of urban pastors who remarked again and again that transportation was a great barrier in the struggles of the underemployed.

Erin and Matt took the lead with finding the way to the Brasserie. They must have hit it at just the right time, for they didn't have to wait to be seated. They were directed to a corner table and sat in dark bentwood chairs beneath colorful poster art.

"This was a good choice," observed Beth when the hostess had left.

"How's your father doing?" asked Davis.

"He's fine," was Matt's reply. "He remarried after I went to college, and lately, he's been talking about early retirement."

Something in the young man's voice told McGowan that while his father might be fine, Matt was not entirely fine with it. Davis let it slide. "How about you two? We know that Erin's here for an interview, but my head's still turning to think that my sixteen-year-old fossil-hunting friend is now married! There are a lot of gaps to fill."

Erin smiled. "Matt said you'd remember his fossil hunting days. We'd never been to Dayton where he grew up, so we drove in from Indianapolis and stopped to see, well… some of the places that are important."

Davis caught the hesitancy in her voice and knew that one of the places was the gravesite where Angie Fornesby was buried. "I assume you went to the cemetery."

"Yes," she said softly, "and to the old house, his school, and the church. It was a very nice visit; I think we really grew closer." She reached to touch Matt's right hand that rested on the table near the frost-glazed water glass.

"The place is really built up around there now," said Matt.

"We've thought the same thing too," remarked McGowan, "you have to look between all the new buildings to see what remains of the town we knew."

Time flowed swiftly as the young couple described their journey. Erin was already an intern when she and Matt met in Indianapolis. He was in an executive trainee program at Lilly. She had graduated from Indiana University School of Medicine's eye institute with a degree in ophthalmology. "Diabetic retinopathy is her specialty," Matt had quickly added.

She was coming to Cleveland to further her work. "It sounds incredible," she said, "but statistically, one in thirteen are affected by the disease." Davis had heard such statistics before, and with increasing weight trends and diabetes on the rise, blindness caused by retinopathy would only increase.

"How about you, Matt? Will you have to leave your job?"

"They aren't happy," Fornesby began, "but they're willing to put me in the trenches for awhile. They're going to let me be a primary sales rep in diabetes. At least I'll have an income, not to mention a live-in source of information on diabetes treatment. She's looking at a residency position. That will only be a few years and Indy isn't that far if they want me closer. Who knows? Maybe something will come of all the medical mart plans that Cleveland has been touting. I might be in a position to become my company's point person on that project."

"I've driven by your company's headquarters many times," said McGowan. "Our daughter lives almost in sight of it; just off East Street. She was probably a few years ahead of you in the youth group at church."

It was like the reunion of family members after years of long separation. Davis realized that the emotional content of his career, though buried, was not deep beneath the surface. Pastoral ministry carried a sort of schizophrenic set of boundary issues. While serving a congregation, a minister was the accessible authority figure to turn to in time of crisis or need. When a new pastor was installed, it was the duty of his predecessor to evaporate, much to the chagrin of those who valued the companionship of a spiritual mentor or trusted confidant. McGowan always played his part well. Even in retirement he had moved 180 miles away from the familiar turf of his Presbytery. Still, there were people who called or wrote, but he played by the rules that forced memory and friendship into a small corner of his brain.

He and Beth had left the parish early, and against the complaints of colleagues who thought him a competent leader. "Just because you are good at something, doesn't mean you have to do it forever," he often said. The truth was that he feared losing his soul to a role. Beth had seen it, and even started to believe that she was merely "the minister's wife" and not her own person. They decided to go to a place where they would just be people.

It was a good plan, but now Davis found himself in the city of his youth, and tagged *it* by his professional past. If Matt Fornesby's sudden appearance revitalized past memories and relationships, the spires across the street were a reminder of the fact that his role as a minister was still entwined with his sense of self. Maybe it was not the *role* at all, but the values that permeate belief and his persistently naïve hope that people with a common purpose could make the world a better place.

He must have been staring blankly because Beth had to say his name twice to draw him out of his reverie. "Davis, Erin wants to know how long you are going to be preaching at Old First."

"Sorry," he said, "I guess I got hit by a lot of memories all at once. Old First? I have a one-year contract, but that can be terminated with thirty days notice."

"Sounds kinda brutal," said Speer.

"Not at all," protested Davis. "They are looking for a full-time pastor, and I'll be more than happy to have that done sooner, rather than later. I'd like to get back into retirement where Beth and I are just *that couple* who always walk around town. Don't get me wrong; Old First is a great church with a long history...it's just that, well, I have a long history too and they need someone a little newer."

"I doubt that," interrupted Matt. "You were the right person when my mother died. I'm older now, and maybe can see things better, but you saved my life."

Davis didn't know what to say, so he let his silence speak. He wondered if Matt knew what his father had done for him more than a decade earlier. There is a certain satisfaction that comes when a parent realizes that a young person has successfully navigated the obstacles of adolescence and entered the world of adult fears. Davis had such an awareness as the visit with Matt and Erin rolled along comfortably until the clock on the wall reminded them of time and the outside world. They parted with promises to meet again, either in Cleveland where Dr. Speer would take up a residency or in Indianapolis with dinner in a downtown restaurant.

"If you end up looking for a house," McGowan advised, "I'm sure you'll be pointed toward the east side. Just remember, it snows a *lot* more on the high ground east of Cleveland." Where they would choose to live would probably be based on which campus of the University Circle Hospital would be the site of Erin's practice and not a matter of the reality of the Snow Belt.

Still, as a Westsider, Davis felt an obligation to get in his dig. Commuters from the west got the morning sun and the drive into town. Eastsiders got snowcapped mountains at every intersection and driveway. Which was preferable? McGowan had his personal preference, but the divided city could only agree that trying to build a couple of blocks north the Square would be out of the question.

"What did you think about what Matt said?" asked Beth on the drive back to their home in Huron.

"About what?"

"About you as the right person."

Davis found the same silence he had earlier, but this one came of the fear that his voice might betray emotion. But this was Beth. "Made me think that I did a few things right."

"More than a few."

Chapter 17

Emerging Issues

Darnell was still trying to piece together a plan to stop a murder that might not even be committed. In the back of his mind was the growing awareness that as much help as Megan had been, the task of anticipating a serial killer's next random visit was less likely than winning the lottery. What he was even more conscious about was the simple truth that he wanted to meet with Megan Sorento again, preferably without any precinct agenda. The complications of that thought were emotionally confusing, not because of any personal doubts but because they always danced around any issue of race. Being partners on a case was an easy pairing. Wiping a tear without thinking was simply an inadvertent gesture of common humanity. To touch her hand gently without an intention of letting go was beyond the barriers of proper copdom. Even so, as the argument went within himself, they were not from the same department or jurisdiction, none of the rules applied.

And yet, unspoken barriers might have more power than the city's personnel policy handbook. They were Black Baptist and Irish-Italian Catholic. He argued to himself that this was, after all, the twenty-first century and officially these barriers had fallen long ago. Experience told Darnell that the unofficial line between public correctness and private opinion, however, could be vicious. The *modern attitude toward ethnic tolerance* was, at times, simply an idiomatic expression meaning *go ahead and hate, just don't say anything out loud.* It worked both ways white *and* black, not white *or* black. Of course *Asian, Hispanic, Muslim,* and *Jew* could be the modifier along with a host of others.

His cell phone broke the reverie of doubt, but only for an instant, until the screen identified Megan Sorento as the caller. He put on his neutral, steady cop voice. "Hey, Megan. What's up?"

There was a brief pause at the other end. Maybe it wasn't Megan, just someone using her phone. "Darnell," it was she. "Darnell, I need you to be honest."

"I don't think I've been too dishonest," he protested lightly.

"Hey, don't make this harder than it is already."

Wilson wondered what had happened to his usually unflappable partner. "Sorry," he said, "no more joking. What's the trouble?"

"It's Bruce McClelland. Remember you met him when you came down to the Bureau?"

He had seemed like a nice enough guy, thought Darnell. Megan had described him as terminally married. "What did he do?"

"Nothing," said Sorento quickly. "It's just that he's having a cookout on Labor Day and invited me. Told me that I could bring a friend. I said that I really wasn't seeing anyone, and he asked about you."

Bless you, Bruce McClelland. "He doesn't really know much about me."

"Well," Megan paused, "I've asked him some about the case and told him how well we work together. I explained that we were work partners and shouldn't mix duty with personal stuff."

"What did he say to that?"

"He laughed and asked me to refresh his memory as to when the *Company* assigned me to the case and if you had left the Lakewood police."

"Yes," said Darnell.

"You left Lakewood?"

"No, I understand your apprehension; I've had the same questions. My 'yes' is to the picnic. I thought I'd cut short your misery."

"So you think it's okay that we go together, to the McClelland's, that is?"

"I had my doubts, but I will not argue against the upper echelons of the Feds. Would this be considered a *date* or just a *good friend* thing?"

Another pause. "What do you think?"

"Well, I'd prefer a date, but you're the one asking so you get to tag the evidence." He wondered if he had just taken a big risk. Then again, he wasn't in junior high even if something about Megan Sorento made him feel as awkward as he remembered.

"That's what I was thinking," came the reply and Darnell could see the school cafeteria decorated with crepe paper— with the girls on one side and the boys strutting on the other. This was one of those rare, magical moments when two people met in the middle of the room. They had no way of understanding what could come next, but the mixture of relief and exhilaration collided in a quiet sort of assurance.

"We'll talk before then," Megan was saying, "I'll get the details from Bruce and we could meet..."

"I'll pick you up," interrupted Darnell, "you said this was a date!"

"If you want," she replied. (He wanted.) "It's just that he lives south and you'd have to come over to the east side, out of the way."

"Megan Sorento, if you think you're not worth it, just say so. But I think I already have enough evidence to get a conviction. Give me a time and I'll be there."

"Thanks, Darnell. Talk to you soon." With that the call was over, and Wilson had to square his mind with a different reality. The fact was that he was not yet on the city's time clock. He came to the precinct early to meet with Jake Sobieski, the man who became his mentor during his time as a rookie.

Jake was hard-core, at least that's what Wilson thought in the first days when they drove together. "I have a notebook at home," Jake had bragged, "with everybody I ever arrested who got put away." The infamous *notebook* sounded like bravado at first, but over time Wilson understood that it was real. Sobieski had a notebook, several, in fact with every mug shot and report that he had written in thirty years. He also came to learn that it wasn't bravado.

"Some of these guys are scary," he would say. From a six-foot-four potential linebacker, that was not a light comment. "Some of them will do their time thinking of the cop who was there when they were busted and there when they sat in court. An accountant always has a paper trail. My notebooks are my ledger. Somebody comes after me, I'll be going over my former accounts," he said. "And if one of them gets me," he instructed his rookie partner, "you go back and check. Promise me that?"

At the time, it sobered up a young tough named Darnell Wilson. At the precinct there was a fraternity (at that time) of men who could recite Jake's speech verbatim. They teased him about it, but knew it was a truth that haunted every veteran and was carefully imparted to any rookie that had the potential to make it.

"We're not sure of anything about this case," said Darnell, "except that, if my guess is right, we'll find a body of an innocent woman at Edgewater Park just a third of the way into the month of September. She'll be strangled and in the trunk of her own car."

"How are they strangled?" asked Jake.

"If it's the same killer, we've seen three different ligatures. The first one was a video game power cord. The second was a cell phone charger. The third was plastic tubing."

"Tubing?"

"Does that mean something?"

"No, it's just really different. What sort of tubing?"

"The best I can describe is medical tubing. Like from an oxygen tank. You see old people in the grocery stores pushing around those little tanks."

"It makes sense," said Jake. "These guys use something that presents itself from the environment. It sounds to me like this guy is growing up. Graduated from video games to cell phones. Must have some contacts, if he has a phone, but then, I saw a guy one time sitting at the end of a bar talking into a small block of wood that he'd painted to look like a cell phone. Some people don't really need actual contacts; they just want other people to think they have them."

"What about the plastic tubing?"

"Like I said, every guy I've ever dealt with used stuff that was close at hand. Maybe somebody in his small circle was using oxygen. These guys are usually loners, so maybe he works at some low-level job in a hospital or nursing home."

"They found some fibers in one of the cars that turned out to be from those protective booties that people wear in operating rooms with scrubs."

"Well, that narrows it down to about 50,000 people," said Jake. "The plumber who came to cut the roots out of our sewer lines wore those when he came into our house to snake the drains. Those protective booties show up all over the place."

"No shit!" said Darnell.

"Exactly," answered Sobieski, picking up on the joke.

"We know the guy was behind the counter at an area Wallace," said Wilson. "An FBI agent that I've talked to gave me that tidbit. A print lifted from one of the cars at Edgewater matched a *John Doe* that was on file from a snatch-and-run at a drug store."

"Those guys are an easy catch."

"That's the point, they caught the guy who jumped the counter, but they weren't his prints. And, no one else's that worked in the pharmacy," added Darnell.

"I never saw a pharmacist in scrubs, did you?" asked Jake. "White coats, but not scrubs. I take that back, in the ER anyone can have sterile gear, but not in a retail shop. What do you think?"

"I think Jake Sobieski is a frickin' Polish genius!"

"Would you write that in a note for my wife?"

"Wife, children, or grandchildren sure!" said Wilson. "Unless the pharmacy had their sewers back up, there must be somebody on their staff that wears the occasional foot protection."

"Hey, I am a genius," agreed Jake. "Someday I'll have to invite you over to see my notebook."

"Jake, I'd love to come over, but I've seen your notebooks. As impressive as they are, they scare the hell out of me."

"Does your FBI agent friend have anything to match it?"

Darnell could feel his face flush.

"I've heard that she's a looker," commented Sobieski.

"Is there anything you don't know?" asked Wilson.

"A few things, I have my sources. What is your next move?"

"This investigation is completely off the record, so when I get a day off, I'll pay a visit to my local pharmacy and see how they dress for work. The pharmacy staff at the time were all eliminated. They all agreed to being printed, but someone else must have been behind the counter, maybe a contractor. Maybe they had their sink drains snaked. It's a long-shot. There's probably no one around who remembers the robbery, but they may be able to say if someone wears surgical booties when they come to work."

"I think that's a good move," agreed Sobieski, "but I was asking about your next move with FBI."

Darnell smiled broadly. "I like her a lot."

"How about her? I'll bet she carries an automatic and knows how to use it!"

"We've been sort of walking around personal stuff, but she just asked me to go to a picnic at her supervisor's house."

"Her supervisor? That's just one level away from mom and dad."

"Do you think I'm being stupid or naïve, Jake?"

"Well, I've been told that I'm a frickin' genius, and I think it's right if you two think it's right. That's the difference between us. I was cursed with great intelligence and you took all the good looks!"

"You know what I'm talking about. I'm being serious."

Jake looked square into Darnell's face. "I have notebooks full of mug shots of bad guys who decided to cross all kinds of lines to get what they wanted. If you want to be scared of the reaction of the nuts, I can show you reams of evidence. I guess I tend to think of us cops as the ones who are willing to get into the faces of the creeps and say 'try me.' Sometimes they'll come out shooting, but mostly they're going to roll over. If you two want it to work, it will. If they do come out, though, make sure you call for backup. You've got a lot of friends, Wilson."

"Thanks, Jake."

Chapter 18

Vietnam

"Davis, I have a problem."

McGowan looked toward the door of his office where Colleen McQuisten stood. It was the first time he had ever heard her call him by his given name, at least without his correcting her usual "Dr. McGowan."

"Come on in," he said, "what's wrong?"

"It's Burt," she said. "He's coming out of the hospital and he's going to need some help at home." Colleen sat down in one of the upholstered chairs that sat opposite the oak desk. McGowan rose from behind the desk and took the chair next to where she now sat.

"In other words, he's not following doctor's orders and checking into rehab."

"What? And sink the *Booker T*?"

Davis grinned at the reference. "No, I guess he couldn't. What does he need?"

"Well, he says that he's ready to lay in the course and he needs me to be the designated helmsman."

"And you understand what he means?"

"Aye, aye," barked Colleen. "I've lived upstairs from Burt and Helen for most of my life now. She was the sweetest woman; they were both like parents to me. That was more than forty years ago."

"That's longer than you worked at the church," commented Davis.

"Helen and Burt were the ones who helped me get the job. Some thought the whole idea of hiring me was scandalous." The look on McGowan's face told her that she had to fill in some gaps. He understood that at an earlier time in her life, what she was saying would have been akin to the confessional, but now she spoke of her past without a hint of remorse. This was her life and there was just no room for the baggage of old guilt.

"I was sixteen when I got pregnant. Jerry and I were both kicked out of high school. He did 'the right thing' as it was called. We got married, and he went into the marines. (He just turned eighteen when he went into basic.) Anyway, that was when Vietnam was getting hotter. We didn't have much time together before Bobby was born and then Jer was in the jungle. We didn't have too many options at the time. Our families were convinced that we'd ruined our lives, and they washed their hands. We needed a place to live, somewhere cheap but safe."

"Burt and Helen?" Davis added.

"Yes, Burt and Helen. I'd guess that Burt has told you something about the war, but not how he landed so far inland. He doesn't tell that part to many. I'll just say, they knew tough times and he was mad at anybody he saw as two-faced. He was more outspoken in those days."

Davis laughed.

"I guess not," she continued, "he's pretty much the same. Calls a spade a spade. Anyway, he called out our families and rented us the other half of the double they had just converted. The rent was ridiculously low, but he said that I could make up for it by helping Helen. She had a baby, too. They started late. Hugh and Bobby were more like brothers than anything else. I suppose it was lucky seeing as how they were both 'only children,' they just didn't know it."

"What about your husband?"

"He came back a couple of times, from the war, I mean. He was wounded, but he always managed to go back. He'd say stuff like, 'the shrapnel will help me stay under when I'm hiding in a rice paddy.' He'd always laugh after that."

"How did you feel?"

"It really scared me. Sometimes I thought that he wanted just to die like his buddies. I thought maybe he felt guilty about being alive. Believe me I've heard all the psychology-talk. Then there were all the war protesters. I just wanted my old boyfriend back, but he never came home."

"He was killed?"

"No, changed. He looked good, but he got called 'village burner' and 'baby killer' and a whole lot of things. Burt talked to him. When he got back from World War II, the merchant mariners were called 'Communists' and 'draft dodgers.' Burt knew what Jerry was going through. You do what your country asks and then you're swept out with the trash. Jerry used stronger language to describe the feeling."

"What happened to him?"

"He couldn't stand it when it was quiet. Seems funny, now. You can sit out in the evening during summer and hear the constant noise of traffic. There are always people around, but Jerry would get panicky. He'd be drinking and you could sense he was building up to it. He'd say, 'we'd put these claymores around the perimeter so that we could blow off the Vietcong when they tried to crawl into camp at night.' Claymores were some sort of mines. Then he'd bring down his gun. He wasn't supposed to have one. He'd sometimes shoot it at night. Cops were always called out. They understood as much as anyone.

"One time he was bragging on *his friend*, that's what he called his M16, he said 'she didn't like being quiet and couldn't always be trusted to keep her mouth shut.' One time, he said he was in the back of a truck and they were driving along a dirt road. *She* was sitting on his lap when an old man on a bicycle passed by going the other way. 'Wouldn't you know it,' he said, 'she blew a fart just as the old guy cleared the truck's ass, and he just flew away.'" Colleen went silent.

"Do you know what he meant?" asked Davis.

"He killed the old man for no reason," she said. "That's what he was telling me, but he wasn't like that. He was a sweet, gentle boy who was lowered into hell on a chain, and then was yanked back into civilian life. One night he was really drunk. He shot the neighbor's dog. It was barking and he thought it would give away our position. They issued a warrant, and he took a couple hundred dollars and went to Florida. He was living in a trailer near the Everglades for awhile. The Lakewood police didn't push the issue. A lot of them were vets and they knew that the war had really killed Jerry. They were the ones who came to tell me that his body was found in a swamp."

"What happened?" asked Davis.

"Who knows? I always imagined that he was hiding from the Vietcong. I was working at the church by then. Helen and Burt stood by me. Burt insisted that Jerry would be buried with full honors at a national cemetery. If anyone suggested otherwise, well, he would roll up his sleeves and face the *Booker T. Washington*. At that time, the only national cemetery in Ohio was in Dayton, so we went down there and had a graveside service. Both our families came, the boys, and, of course, Helen and Burt. Jerry wasn't Catholic, but the minister at Old First called a church near the cemetery in West Dayton. I'll never forget the minister's kindness. He was an African-American, name of *Jones*, and he was from the College Hill congregation.

"Robert E. Jones," corrected Davis.

"Do you know him?"

"I do. Among other things, we worked together at a neighborhood center. I liked him very much. He's my mentor for urban ministry, even if he did go to Yale Divinity School. Sorry," said Davis, "that was one of our inside jokes."

Colleen reached for a tissue from the box that sat on the edge of McGowan's desk. "I don't know why I'm telling you all this except maybe it will help you understand why I am so caught between my work and Burt. He's my father, or might as well be. He makes what I think might be unreasonable demands, but I still can't turn my back on him. He wants to come home in three days. Dr. Shafer says that they really can't keep him any longer at the hospital. He could go to rehab, but he's refusing."

"And you are *the girl upstairs* who is going to take care of him. Sorry, that's what Burt said to me before I knew he was talking about you."

"That's right. The hospital has made arrangements for someone to come out to the house to see how we can set up everything so he can get to the bathroom and such. I think we'll be turning the dining room into a hospital room and getting some sort of potty chair until he can get around better. There's hardwood flooring there and they seemed to think that important."

"It is. He won't be very mobile and rugs and carpet have a way of tripping up the elderly. Are they going to give him therapy?"

"Yes, three times a week to start with, and he'll get exercises to do in between. I don't worry about that. Burt is strong. He prides himself on that. Of course he's not as strong as he thinks. In his mind, he could take on *almost anyone* in a fair fight, and *anyone at all* in a fight where he could cheat." The two laughed.

"Sounds like Zacharias," agreed McGowan, "and it sounds like you are working through all the details. I'm sure we could line up people to sit with him to relieve you."

"It's not that," said Colleen cautiously. "And please, don't say this to Burt. I have to think about moving."

"Moving?"

"Not right away, but, this is hard to say, all of a sudden, I realized that I'm losing him. As much as we've depended on each other like father and daughter, he's still my landlord. When he passes... well, I have to have it thought out. I don't want him to know, his only concern should be to get well. I want to keep him, but I have to be realistic.

"Anyway, you've met Rachel, the wait over at John Q's." Davis nodded, and she continued. "We've been friends since high school. She stuck with me through my ordeal. Her husband was in Nam too. He came home and seemed in better shape than Jerry, but had a lot of health problems. She pretty much supported the family, and he was in and out of the VA. Had his first stroke when he was only thirty-six and only lasted two years beyond that. They had a daughter, Tracie. She acted out a lot of stuff, but got herself back together, even finished college at *Tri-C*.

"Rachel and I thought that things could be a lot better for both of us if we shared an apartment. Neither of us has a car, so we might share that expense, too."

"But I ran into her on Sunday and she said that you had dropped her off?" asked Davis.

"I did, but like *my* house, *my* car is really Burt's. Now you know the truth of how I have paid *my* way through community college and university for Bobby. My rent is $125 a month."

"Wow," agreed Davis.

"It would be less than that if I hadn't negotiated it up."

"Up?"

"When we first moved in, the rent was $25. When I took the job at the church, I told him that I had to pay more since I wouldn't be able to help Helen as much. Then it went to $75. The last time we bargained, he agreed to take $125 *only* on the basis that I would never ask for an increase again. That was twenty-five years ago. He's really spoiled me, and eventually, the whole thing will crumble. So, Rachel and I are going apartment hunting. We want three bedrooms or maybe a small house. I am going to start paying enough to help her afford it, and I'll be working out a more realistic budget."

"Won't it feel kinda odd to be living in your old place while your friend is living in your new home?"

"The way I look at it is that the new place is my safety valve. I'll be living in the only home I've had for my entire adult life. When I do have to give it up, well, I'll be able to go to an old friend who has heard me cry before, and I won't be imposing."

Davis had to agree that if it didn't make the best sense economically, it made complete sense emotionally. Colleen McQuisten was a marvel in self-reliance and compassion for others. These were traits she had mastered for survival, but he wondered if she understood or let in the affection of those around her who valued only her and not her independence.

She was still speaking when McGowan realized that he had been momentarily lost in thought. "So the day that Rachel and I are planning to look at four places is the day that Burt is going to discharge himself from the hospital."

"I would have suspected that you would have mastered the art of two places at once," said Davis, "you've managed greater miracles from what I can see. No, I'm kidding. I do think that I can help you out here. How about if I deal with Burt?"

"You?"

"Sure. I don't see why I couldn't help Burt get home from the hospital. I can say that you and Rachel have a long-arranged girl-thing going on and that I thought it'd be a good time to collect on some more of his *Booker T. Washington* stories and the conversation he promised me when we first met."

Colleen smiled. "You are both devious and kind, Dr. McGowan. Even though he assigned me the duty of bringing him home, I think he'd be relieved if another guy was there to help with any lifting. You may not have guessed it, but he's a proud man."

"I did get that impression," said Davis. "He's just lucky he has 'a girl living upstairs' at the time in life when his body is starting to betray him."

Chapter 19

An Old Print

The display on the cell phone had told her that it was Darnell calling. In that instant she felt a confused blend of emotions. Was he calling *her* or was he calling Agent Sorento? Her intellect knew the answer; he was calling both, but the presenting issue was a series of unsolved murders.

"Megan, I'm on my way out to Wallace Pharmacy to walk through that snatch-and-run that you told me about."

"That happened years ago, Darnell. What are the odds that anyone on the staff there would have even been around then?"

"I know," he said quickly, "it's just that I talked to Jake Sobieski you wouldn't know him, he was my first partner when I came to Lakewood. He's retired now, but comes into the precinct when his wife gets tired of him around the house." Wilson wished he hadn't made that last remark. "I'm not saying he has a bad marriage," he quickly added, "he is just, well, the most meticulous guy I ever met on the force. Keeps records of all his cases and looks for details."

"Maybe he should write a book," offered Sorento.

"He could," answered Wilson, "anyway, when I told him about fibers in the car and the print found at the robbery, he just pointed out the obvious. He noted that contractors often wear those booties to avoid tracking in dirt. The example he gave was a plumber cleaning out blocked drains."

"Duh," replied Megan, "I should have thought of that. Pharmacies have sinks. I know they have tough restrictions on who goes back there and when, but I'd guess clogged plumbing would be a quickly granted exception."

"I just got off my shift, and thought that I'd try to get there and take a look around. Somebody on the staff will know if booties are the uniform-of-the-day for any of their outside vendors."

"Then all we'd need to do is find out if they ever gain access to the pharmacy. If it was a service call, there'll be a billing record for the store. It might take awhile, but I think we could find, at least the name of a company."

"Maybe you could," said Wilson. "It sounds like accountant's work more than CSI."

"Did I ever tell you that that's what we mostly do at the FBI in Cleveland?" replied Megan.

"Good, I'd rather have you facing painful paper cuts than some drug-hyped creep with a semi-automatic."

"Are you saying…"

"No, agent Sorento, I am not saying anything of the sort. I was talking about Megan who has apparently given over the phone to you." They both laughed. The banter felt good.

"Do you want me to provide backup?" asked Sorento. Darnell looked at his watch. It was already past 9:00.

"I'd love to see you, but by the time you could get here, they'd be closed. I hadn't realized how late it is; you're probably headed off to bed."

"Is this going to become an obscene phone call? 'Are you getting ready for bed?' 'What are you wearing?'"

"No, I just hadn't realized... I didn't mean anything by it," protested Wilson.

"Damn!" she replied. "There goes my fantasy, Detective Wilson!" They both laughed again. "This Monday is the picnic. Are you still able to come?"

"If the bad guys stay quiet," offered Darnell. "I will have put in a long weekend, so I might not be the best company."

"It'll give me a chance to meet Grumpy, then. I already met Happy, and I like him fine." Wilson enjoyed her quick humor. "McClelland lives in Independence, so we'll be headed south on 77. Are you sure you don't want to meet me downtown?"

"No, you promised me a date and Ms. Brown always said that a gentleman walked up to the door and escorted his date to the car. No pulling up and honking."

"I like that Ms. Brown. Someday I'd like to meet her."

"Maybe you will," offered Darnell, "maybe you will."

* * * *

It was 9:30 by the time that Wilson pulled into the parking lot at the pharmacy. He sat for a few minutes to watch the traffic patterns. There was a constant movement of cars and light trucks pulling in and out. Some patrons never made it into the store; instead they played with the buttons on the red kiosk of the video rental and then swiped their debit cards. Others moved quickly into and out of the store emerging with the same white paper bags bearing the amber vials of whatever medication that they had waited until the last minute to pick up. Some few came out burdened like mall shoppers with cases of soda and plastic bags stretched grotesquely by the square corners of cardboard boxes.

When he walked through the automatic sliding doors, he was greeted with a "Good evening" and a offer to help find merchandise. For the moment he was fine and nodded to the chunky dark-haired woman who had spoken.

He looked over the countertops for an indication as to the direction of the pharmacy counter. It was in the back and apparently the most direct path was a circuitous trail past greeting cards, laxatives, water purifiers and toaster ovens. The store was spotless and every aisle was capped with an end-unit promoting a sale price too good to pass.

Wilson passed them all.

His education began when he saw a pharmacy technician standing at the register in blue surgical scrubs. His immediate curiosity was what footwear she had on. He wanted to step close enough to look over the counter, but there was a rope barrier indicating where the next in line was to stand, and there were four ahead.

Cutting in front might generate a riot and flashing a badge seemed over a little over-the-top given that he was, as he had said to the Goth clerk, "just looking." He did not have to wait long, however, when a second technician from behind the counter said to the person at the register, "I can help you find that."

In an instant she was walking out through the half-glassed security door with its keypad entry lock. Darnell's gaze went immediately to her feet. There were typical thick-soled jogging shoes, not protective surgical booties.

He turned back toward the main body of the store where the tech led a forty-something woman to the sterile rinse in the eye care area. He heard, "And you can check that out at the front register when you're done shopping, and the interchange was complete. He met her as she headed back to the pharmacy.

"Excuse me," he said, "is there a manager in the store?"

"The manager isn't here right now, but Mr. Wozniak is on duty, he's an EXA," she added as if the company jargon was perfectly understood English. Wilson had no idea of what species an "EXA" might represent, but he did understand "on duty."

With the same helpfulness he had just seen with a customer, she led him back to the front of the store by a side aisle which eliminated the twists of his foray in.

"There he is," she said pointing to a young man wearing a tie and talking with the dark-haired clerk who had greeted him on entering the store.

"Thanks." As he walked toward the man, he overheard a few words.

"Heather, this isn't the first time I've had to tell you this." The young woman seemed blank. Whatever had been spoken, it wasn't the first time, probably not the second or third either. What was clear was that he cared more than she did.

"Mr. Wozniak?" said Wilson.

"Yes, may I help you?"

"I am Detective Wilson of the Lakewood Police," he began. This time he did show his shield and held it out long enough to let Wozniak see that it wasn't something he bought on ebay. "I am doing an informal follow-up to a theft that happened here three years ago. Actually, that case was solved, but there was a loose end, so to speak, that may have an impact on an investigation that I'm doing right now."

Darnell didn't worry about the confusion on Wozniak's face. He had just used a zigzag in the hopes that it would sound a little like a reasonable explanation. He was not really on an assigned case at all, and knew that he'd have a tough time defending the use of his badge.

"I'll do what I can, officer. I haven't been here that long, but I have heard about the time that everyone got fingerprinted. It's sort of an in-house legend in the pharmacy."

"Well what I need to know is more about store policy. I notice that some of your pharmacy staff wear surgical scrubs."

"That's a fairly new company change," Wozniak offered.

"Do they or any of your vendors ever wear surgical shoe coverings?"

The assistant manager thought for a moment. "No, that's never been a requirement. I can't imagine that it would even be suggested."

"What about the people from outside who came to work in the store? Have you ever had to call a plumber, for example, to clean out a drain? Plumbers often put them on when they walk into someone's house."

"When we get backed up drains," he offered, "it's from some brainiac that thinks it's funny to put paper towels in the john. We don't generally call a plumber for that. It happens too often."

"Somebody gets to go fishing, huh?" said Darnell.

"Could say that. Pretty messy, and not my favorite job."

"I suppose that the stink is what keeps people shelling out for expensive drain cleaning. Anyway, if you think of any service people who come in here, would you give me a call?" He handed Wozniak a business card with his precinct number.

"Sure, I'll call," he studied the card, and then turned toward Heather who was standing near the front register. "Heather, do you remember ever seeing any outside vendors in here with surgical shoe coverings?"

"No, Mr. Wozniak," she answered, "but I don't always have the best memory." The assistant manager threw her a momentary glare, and then looked at Wilson.

"I guess not," he said, "but I'll call if anything comes to mind."

By the time Darnell walked out the sliding glass doors, it was nearly ten. Wozniak's voice came over the store's PA system that all but the front register was closed and that guests should make their final selections. "It's a lot like the last call at a bar," thought Wilson. The parking lot was not as full as it had been. A white van was in the space near the front door, and Darnell could see the soft red glow of a cigarette being inhaled by a shadow in the front seat, undoubtedly, the nicotine-addicted partner of some late shopper. He called Megan on his cell phone. He wanted to hear her voice. He really had nothing to add to the case, but he rationalized that she might be staying awake until he gave some sort of report.

"Dead end," he said. "No pun intended," he added, thinking of the *nothing* they had to go on, and the fact that September 10th was less than a week away.

* * * *

"What did you do now, Dickybird?" asked Heather as she walked out to the driver's side of the white van.

"What do you mean?" asked Kosten.

"Nothing. Just that there was a cop in here asking Wozniak if anyone working in the store ever wore surgical booties. I don't know," she added, "it just sounded like you."

Kosten's heart knocked against his chest cavity like a panicky squirrel trying to escape a cage. He held his voice steady, however, and even managed a laugh. "I don't even park illegally," he said.

"If you want to hear something to laugh about, dumb-ass Wozniak couldn't think of anyone who ever wore them." She bent over to feign picking up some litter and carried the non-existent trash back to the receptacle in front of the door. Then she walked back to the side of the van and continued to pretend scouring the area.

"What are you doing?" Kosten asked.

"I'm putting on a show for an EXA who told me that I was too lazy and needed to be friendlier to our guests. Get this, he comes up to me with his usual stick-in-the-butt attitude and lets me have it. This cop walks over, and, all of a sudden, he's Mr. Nice. When he goes blank over the bootie question, he turns and asks me."

"What did you say?"

"Hey, I'm not going to rat out my Dickybird now, am I? Besides if he hasn't ever paid attention to what's going on in his store, who am I to show him up? I am just the lazy-Goth-chick with the tramp stamp!"

"Well, thanks then. Not that I can imagine that the guy was looking for me. It's just that I'd probably have to go through a lot of hassles to prove that I've got nothing to hide and I'm no one they'd want to see."

"I know that, I just think it's funny that the Wizard of Woz is clueless as usual. Better get back inside in case he's watching me over one of the cameras. Maybe he's got a thing for me, that's why he can't stay away. Do you think?"

"Well, I couldn't blame him if he had the hots for you. Just don't pay any attention to the man behind the curtain! Who came up with the Wizard of Woz?"

"That would be me, black mascara and all!"

"That's why I love you, Heather."

"And you'll always be my Dickybird." With that she retreated into the store.

He liked the way Heather walked. It was troubling that she knew about his shoe coverings, but she wouldn't tell Wozniak, at least not tonight. Still, she might say something in an explosive outburst. He could hear her saying, "I'm not the one who's not paying attention! At least I know who covers his shoes when he's working here!" Richard would have to be her Dickybird tonight, but something else might have to be worked out later.

He did not cover his shoes when he buffed the aisles. Several times he caught the Wizard watching him work. Richard wondered if it was just to see if Heather would make her usual moves toward him, so he could write her up. Once, he thought Wozniak was looking at his shoes. Fortunately, he was wearing light colored soles and didn't have to go back over his own scuff marks.

Chapter 20

Two Sons

Davis' offer to play taxi during Zacharias' return home was not entirely a deal between Colleen and himself. Dr. Katherine Shafer had also been in on the scheme. She knew that Burt was not the best at taking orders from the women in his household, but he understood chain of command from his service in the merchant marine. She had noticed in conversations during her rounds as a physician, that Burt's comments about McGowan placed him in the officer corp.

"The hospital will arrange transportation to his house," she noted, "but after they leave, he'll conclude that the restrictions they gave were over-cautious."

"Has he always been this cantankerous?" asked Davis.

Shafer grinned. "Pretty much, but I think it's gotten worse since Helen died. It happens to us all, I guess. We harden into all our personal preferences, and what we want becomes the universal standard that should apply to everyone else."

"Creepy, isn't it? I mean, you and I might be headed that way, too. I suppose that the saving grace is that our opinions *really do* apply to everyone else."

"You betcha," she said mimicking a momma grizzly. "I represent all the medical advances of the modern era, and you are all God. Between the two of us, we've got'em, birth to death and beyond!"

"So, it's a sickness in your profession as well," said McGowan.

"You mean physicians who think they are God? No, I take that back, *who know* that they are the givers of life, and that the death of their patient is due to the ineptitude of the nurse, the resident, or the aide who dumped the bedpan. I have encountered a few," she said.

"They have nothing on the ministers. We bury the mistakes of the docs, or so the saying goes. We get to stand up in front of crowds and tell them, in our own words, what God is saying. After a while some of us forget the part about being *our own words.*"

"Does it scare you that we could be moving in that direction?" asked Shafer.

"It's one of the reasons I retired early. Funny, isn't it that people think that the threat to a minister is to lose his or her faith? The real threat is that they become a caricature of a pious certainty that tramples over the vulnerable."

"Why do you think that happens?"

"I think it happens gradually, like Burt whose physical toughness left a long time ago, and he tries to compensate by talking tougher than his body will allow. I don't know about you docs, but we ministers see a lot of destructive behavior. I suppose we're like frustrated parents who try to be more effective by yelling louder."

"Does that work?" Katherine asked.

"Not with the kids. It works on some religious types, though. You can get them to go out and crusade against all the wrong things in the name of God. I suppose it feels better to get a group together who will shout and protest against evils that are mostly imaginary rather than trying to deal with the mentally ill who live under bridges."

"I think physicians are the same," added Shafer. "Eventually, we're going to lose all our patients even if it's at a ripe old age. Death has become the benchmark, and every success is only relative."

"How did we get on this uplifting topic?" asked McGowan.

"It's Burt's fault for being grumpy," said Katherine. "But he's not too far gone. He's not much afraid for himself, other than the fear of being useless."

"So, I follow the ambulance to his house and make sure he understands the drill."

"That's about it. You know how it goes; he'll want to jump out of bed and go. You have to have him sit up, place both feet squarely on the floor and equalize his weight between his feet on the floor and his arms on the walker. He does have good upper body strength, for his age."

"Okay, when I see him, I'll say, 'Dr. Shafer says you're buff! That should boost his ego."

"McGowan, you're trouble!"

* * * *

Davis heard male voices cascading from Zacharias' room. When he walked in, he saw two men; he guessed they were in their late thirties or early forties.

"Speaking of the devil," cried Burt. "McGowan, I want you to meet my boys. This one is Bobby," he said gesturing to a ginger-haired, red-faced man in a green polo shirt. "And this is Hugh."

Hugh had dark hair and the same sharp features as his father. He rose and offered Davis his outstretched hand.

"Dr. McGowan, we've heard a lot about you. Thanks for taking such good care of my Dad."

"I don't think I've done very much," he answered. He turned his gaze toward Bob, "I work for your mother, and she put me up to it."

"Mom puts us all up to a lot of things," he answered. "It's what she's good at!" The three erupted into good-natured laughter that told Davis that Colleen was as appreciated inside her family as much as at the office.

"I'll attest to that. She and Dr. Shafer have enlisted me to be your father's escort home."

"What's that?" asked Zacharias.

"Actually, I volunteered," McGowan added, "Burt owes me a drink and some stories about the merchant marine."

"Sounds like you, Dad," added Hugh, "trying to turn the minister into one of your drinking buddies."

The room had taken on a party atmosphere, and Davis was glad that the second bed in the room was empty. If Zacharias intended to send up a protest, his complaint was dashed by Hugh's retort. If Davis was okay with providing support for the ride home, he was too. "You volunteered? It had to be a setup," he said.

"Well, think of it," McGowan began, "Old First can get along fine without me for a few hours. Could you say the same of Colleen?" General agreement floated through the laughter. Burt was one of those men who communicated through banter and skirted the deep emotions that powered his life's work in spite of his crusty exterior. Davis understood the type. Truth was that fluency in the language of emotions was a part of his professional package. When it came to talking about himself, however, like Zacharias, he hid behind the screen of rapid deflection. He knew that it was not the best interpersonal stance, but it was the one he had adopted from childhood, and it had become his second nature.

Seeing Hugh, Bobby, and Burt together was an epiphany. Colleen had said that the two *boys* were like brothers, but that attribute is easily, and often wrongly, thrown out for two people who spend years in proximity. With these it would have been impossible to tell from their actions which was the son and which was the renter's son. The three did become serious and quiet when Davis offered a prayer around the bed. It was one of those rare moments in the company of men when silence acknowledged the truth that is constantly slurred in the war of male/female humor. The brunt of most jokes is either the man as a lout or the woman as a bimbo. The hidden irony in such humor is the essence of the lie that each sex's dialect of emotion is unknowable by the other. In this room, there was no correcting voice telling them to "be serious, Burt is at a desperate transition in his life." They all knew that and were working through it as men often do. It would not be tolerated by a psychoanalyst, but none was present and Burt would have thrown one out.

Davis knew the men were working through the emotions of saying their goodbyes when Hugh followed him out the door and walked him to the elevator.

"I meant it when I thanked you for helping my Dad."

"It's really not a problem," answered Davis, "I like him."

"I don't know who really came up with the idea that you get him settled at home. He doesn't like a lot of fussing, and that's what Colleen would do. She really wouldn't fuss that much, it's just that Dad would complain that way."

"I resemble the type," confessed Davis. "Have you spoken to Dr. Shafer?"

"Yes. She told us that he really should be going to rehab, but…"

"But she knows your father."

"Exactly. Anyway, Bob and I knew that we had to get here, and the Labor Day weekend was the excuse to counter Dad's protests. He puts duty above everything else, and doesn't want to think of himself as number one on the Bob and Hugh duty roster."

"Do you think he understands his situation?" asked Davis.

"He made it a point to tell us both where he keeps his will and the name of his attorney."

"Sounds ominous."

"No, he wasn't morbid. It was more like, 'and don't forget to scoop Colleen's cat's litter box.'" The two laughed.

Davis reached into the breast pocket of his blazer and pulled out a business card. He handed it to Hugh. "Don't be afraid to call me. My home and cell number are there. The truth is that if anything happens to your father, Colleen may be the one who will need the support."

"That's very true. I'll call Bob and you before I call her. Then again, she might be right there."

"She usually is," answered Davis. "She seems to be the go-to person for a lot of folks. The problem is that if anything happens to Burt, she'll be facing a lot of changes for herself."

"I know," agreed Hugh. "Bob and I have talked about it. He teaches history at Youngstown State, and would really like her to come down there."

"That ain't going to happen," said Davis.

"I know. Dad is tight-lipped about the whole thing. He just says he's already made up his mind. Told us to just dump the body overboard, and have the captain say a prayer after the decks are hosed down."

"Whoa, that's pretty grizzly," offered McGowan.

"I think it's just what he saw as a young man. He's seen more than he ever talked about. He's not afraid to die."

"And you, Hugh Mulzac Zacharias, are you the captain? You carry the captain's name."

"Not this time," said Zacharias, "I think that duty falls to you." The elevator door opened and Hugh's hand met Davis'. When they broke the handshake, Hugh gave a stone-faced salute and turned quickly before McGowan could see the salt water in his eyes.

Chapter 21

Independence

Bruce McClelland lived in a comfortable home that backed onto an expanse of woods that was the outer perimeter of the Cuyahoga Valley National Park. Megan served as the navigator and they exited I-77 at Pleasant Valley Road. On the return home, they took the more locally trafficked route north on Brecksville Road.

"It can't be too much farther," said Darnell, "that big intersection ahead has to be Rockside."

"And there it is," said Megan, "the elegant two-story McDonald's. You take me to the best places. First the Blue Point in Cleveland and now the *Golden Arches*."

"Bruce was taking a lot of ribbing for being out here in Independence, and a McDonald's with a chandelier was the proof. Took me awhile to figure out what they were talking about." He pulled into the lot from the northbound lane of Brecksville Road. "Do we dare go in?" he asked.

"Dare? A cop and an FBI agent?"

"You know what I mean," said Wilson.

"Actually, I don't. You've seemed a little off-balance all day. Oh, you were fine when you picked me up at my condo, and the farther south we went on 77, the more nervous you got. Once you got into the mood of the picnic, you were great. Now, I feel you getting tense again. Do you not like my friends?"

For some reason, Darnell had not expected such directness from Megan. *But why not?* He asked himself, *she's a cop, too*. He thought he had been pretty much in control of his demeanor, but she saw through him.

"Your friends are great," he said at last, "I was afraid that they might not accept me. When they were polite, at first, I thought they must really like you, but I was wrong."

"You think they don't like me?" said Sorento, taunting.

"No, I don't mean that at all. They really like you. I just thought that they were being nice to me because I was with you, but I was wrong. They were genuinely good people."

"Darnell, you fit in just fine."

"I know that now," he said, "but there's a lot of fear that gets put in your head growing up. It's not dumb stuff, it's real. I am a cop. I can go anywhere under the protection of my badge and hold my own against anyone. When I take off the badge, well, we were taught to lock the car doors when we drove out of the city."

"And we locked our doors in the city," offered Sorento.

"Exactly," said Wilson, "our brains get loaded with the fears of others. My cousin worked as a custodian in a church just outside of Columbus. He was picked up seven times over the years he worked there. He'd go in early on Mondays to put out the trash and get challenged for handling the trash cans."

"So you're afraid to be caught unaware at a McDonald's in an upper middle class suburb? The world has changed, Darnell Wilson. Haven't you heard? The President of the United States is black."

"Funny, I heard he was half-white." Wilson's words had left his lips before they could be measured.

"Touché," said Megan. "But you can't tell me that you are afraid to walk into Mickey D's. You are afraid to walk in there with me."

"I..." Darnell was caught off-guard.

"Darnell, at some point I thought we'd need to have a talk. I didn't think it would be before we finished the first date at a McDonald's." She reached across to touch where his hand rested on the steering wheel. "Let's look up at the chandelier and get a couple of coffees to go."

"I'm afraid, Megan; not for me, but for you. The world has changed, but there are still people who say all the right words but look for you later in a lonely place."

"Bring 'em on. I went to the FBI to root out the small-minded turds of this world. I find a guy that I like and he might be a closet wuss. Are you going to let me buy you a coffee?" She opened her door and put a foot on the blacktop. Darnell's reflexes put him less than a millisecond behind.

"Look, Sorento, I may not be with the Bureau, but I've been on the frontlines, and I'm no wuss!"

Megan burst out laughing, and Wilson joined her. "Okay," she said, "didn't think you were. You said it before, cops are tough to date. They have guns and scare the crap out of even law-abiding citizens at times. Let's not try to scare each other; what do you say?"

"Let's go in together, Megan. By the way, how do you like your coffee?"

"With you."

* * * *

The McDonald's was out of the ordinary, at least on the count of the over-the-top architecture. On the other hand, the menu was strictly *golden arches* with the ordinary menu and prices.

"I've heard that *presentation* is one of the most important ingredients in gourmet restaurants," said Wilson.

"Before I agree, I need to make a general statement," responded Sorento. "Fast food is for quick eating, not cheap dating."

"Never mind," said Darnell. Their laughter turned heads as they walked into what could only be described as a vestibule.

Megan took his hand. "Just a coffee to go," she said. All the patrons went back to their own business.

"No," he said. "Let's enjoy it here. Don't drink it fast. I want it to count as a part of our first date!"

It was a quite natural reaction when Megan leaned in to rest her head momentarily against his shoulder.

* * * *

"This is not the date that I had anticipated," said Darnell breaking the comfortable silence of the car. "I expected that we'd mostly jabber about September 10th and the fact that we're getting a few pieces, but they don't come together very well. Instead, I got to spend the whole day with Megan. Agent Sorento didn't even show herself until we got to the parking lot."

"She didn't have to come out until then because we were on a date. She had to show herself when that cop guy tried to switch the rules of engagement."

"Hey, this was a first date. What's with the talk of *engagement*?"

"Don't tell me you're one of those commitment-phobic men. But, you're right about two things. One is that we should talk about the case, and the second is that it turned out to be a good date. In case you are wondering McClelland and his wife have given us their stamp of approval. They like you."

"That's two," said Darnell. "Three, if you count me."

"And four, if I get a vote," added Megan. "When do I get to meet your friends, or even better, Ms. Brown?"

Darnell laughed. "I don't have any bring-a-date invitations at the moment, but I'd love to take you to meet Ms. Brown; that can be arranged with a phone call. And, she will like you very much!"

"So, she'll have an open mind?"

"I'm sure."

"Then we're up to five! But you have to promise me one thing, before you make the call."

"What's that?"

"Well, I'm from the Midwest, you know, and we've always been characterized as colloquial and quaint. Before you tell Ms. Brown that I'm your girlfriend, I really want to know if you're a good kisser. You've been pretty standoffish in that department, and there are just some things a girl needs to know. I expect a goodnight kiss, is that okay?"

Darnell tromped on the accelerator in response, and then immediately eased off.

"Careful," she said, "if we get pulled over... well we're out of your jurisdiction and we'd be late getting home."

Chapter 22

Secure Place

No one else had ever been in this room. At least not since he had sound-proofed it and enlarged it to suit his purposes. Initially, it was little more than a walk-in closet with a small desk and a bulletin board. In his younger years, it was a place for schoolwork and a haven to lie low when his mother had been drinking. It could be locked from the inside as well as from without, sometimes both. Several times when he had thrown the bolt against the yelling, he would discover the outer bolt locked against him. On those occasions he learned patience and preparedness. After the first twelve hour stint, he stocked liter bottles of pop, a jar of peanut butter, and a box of saltines. He also had a covered five gallon pail that he had pilfered from the trash when an apartment on Cove Avenue was being renovated. It had contained drywall compound, but that washed out with a hose. Now it served as a commode that would seal tight against the stench of his bowel movements.

Since his mother's death, the space had become an obsession. The sliding bolts were replaced with a keyed deadbolt which was covered, on the outside, by Van Gogh's *Sunflowers*. The door itself was obscured with a floor-to-ceiling wooden panel that seamlessly finished what became a striking accent wall in an otherwise beige bedroom.

Someone with a tape measure and a suspicious mind could have detected a six foot discrepancy between the apartment's interior and the corridor that ran through the center of the building to the back stairwell which added another five feet to the interior of his secure place. The interior was not very elegant. His early attempts at sound-proofing consisted of stapling corrugated cardboard to the wall surfaces and ceiling. Boxes were easily brought in past his mother's scrutiny and the larger ones would lay flat when broken down. As he got older, and had a regular income, he bought acoustical ceiling panels which could be applied with construction adhesive. These also provided a place to mount pictures and newspaper clippings with colored push-pins. Each Rachael was coded with red, green, or yellow. Photographs of the current Rachael were clear, but he had a blister-pack of blue to use when the obituary was filed. He knew that, while he was running out of primary colors, there were pastels on the market. Still, he wondered if it would be better just to stick with these four and create color differentiated sets, but there was still time to decide.

Of more significance was the Lakewood cop that had appeared at the store. He was Heather's Dickybird, but the time was getting close and trust could only go so far. Killing her now could make a real mess of September 10th, but so could a hissy-outburst to the Wizard of Woz. It would be better if she just went away for a few days.

After the 10th he could count on the fact that his thinking would be more clear, and he could fix everything then.

Chapter 23

Home

"He really should have a ramp," the EMT was saying to Davis as they pulled out the gurney from the rear bay door of the ambulance. The lights on the square truck were not flashing. This was not a squad run; it was Burton Zacharias coming home to the first floor of his Lakewood double.

"I'm sure that's on the list," said McGowan. "I think everything is ready on the inside. They've put a hospital bed in the dining room where there are hardwood floors. His bedroom's on the first floor, but it's still the sixties shag carpet." Colleen had walked Davis and Beth through the modifications on Tuesday in preparation for Burt's homecoming. The large walnut table had to be pushed against the wall to make room for the bed and the portable potty-chair. The buffet against the wall was loaded with medications, tissue boxes, and an assortment of plastic containers ranging from an ice pitcher to a blue kidney-shaped spit cup and an opaque urinal. Beth was at the "orientation" because she had offered to spell Colleen on days when her work schedule did not conform to Zacharias' therapy regime. On this Wednesday, however, Davis was alone, ostensibly to hear about the *Booker T*; in reality it was to deflect embarrassment, fear, anger, or any other emotion that could erupt from a fiercely proud man whose body was betraying him.

"It was good to meet Hugh and Bobby the other day," Davis offered. Burt looked a little fearful as the attendants slid the gurney out from the truck body and the wheeled-legs extended.

"Getting safely dockside is always the dangerous part," he observed. "Much safer out in open water."

Davis understood his meaning. "I think these guys have done this before," he said.

"Only a few thousand times," said the large man with a reddish buzz cut, the one who had made the comment about needing a ramp.

"Always good to have a pilot who's familiar with the waters," said Zacharias. Even for Burt the use of the nautical language was on the heavy side, and McGowan wondered if the oral morphine was making him a little giddy.

"We'll have you in your bed, safe and sound soon enough, Mr. Zacharias," said the woman attendant. She was stocky with great upper body strength judging from the way she swung her end of the gurney around to face square on to the front door.

Davis quickly pulled open the screen and slid the metal tab on the door closer to lock it open. "Enjoying the ride?" he asked Zacharias as he floated by. It was clear that he was not.

The two EMTs did not waste much time transferring their patient to the bed. With practiced efficiency and teamwork, they set the narrow gurney against the right side of the bed. The man crossed around until the bed, the gurney and Burt were between him and his partner. On the count of three they lifted the old man on the blue striped blanket that was beneath him. With one swift tug, Burt was centered on the bed and being rolled side to side so that the blanket could be pulled out from beneath him. It reminded Davis of the magician who could pull the tablecloth off a set dining room table and not leave a glass wobbling. The end of this trick was Zacharias resting comfortably.

"Wow, they didn't give you enough time to wince," observed McGowan.

"They do know what they're doing. It's like a good crew coming into harbor. Never much talking needed, it's everyman at his station doing what he's been trained to do," said Burt.

"*I'm sorry*," said the female attendant.

"I'm an old sailor," said Zecharaias, "not used to having women onboard, but I could get used to it. You do good work!"

"Are you trying to hit on me, Mr. Zacharias?"

"Bet I'm not the only one," he confessed.

"This guy's fine," she said to her partner. "I think our work is done here, Robin."

"Does that make you *Batman*?" asked Burt without hesitation.

"Watch it, old man," she said, "is that another of your sexist remarks?" Davis wondered what conversation must have taken place in the ambulance that the three already were bantering freely.

"The fact is," said the male driver, "that my name is *Robin* and she knows that I hate it. So you just keep calling her *Batman* and maybe she'll call me *Rob* like she's supposed to."

The woman turned to Davis. "You can see why it's so hard to be a superhero these days."

"I have exactly the same problem," said Davis, and the four shared a good laugh.

The paperwork was brief but thorough with all the legal loopholes closed, and both Davis and Burt thanked the team as they gathered all their equipment and headed out, releasing the screen door as they left. Alone in the house, they went over the checklist of symptoms, the do's and don'ts of eating, drinking, resting, sitting up, getting up, and passing BMs.

"I thought that I had mastered all this when I was two," said Burt. "Now they want me to learn it all again."

"Maybe it's a second childhood coming on?" said Davis.

"Doesn't feel *that* good. When I was a kid it was easier to get away with stuff. These hospital people are tougher than parents!" Zacharias tried to lift his right leg to cross his ankles."

"I don't think you are supposed to cross your legs," warned Davis.

"So, you are one of them!"

"Well, I have known a lot of people with hip and knee replacements. No crossed legs, no twisting to get out of cars, you've heard it all. Just so you know, the ones who don't follow orders get to go back to the hospital and get refitted."

"Damn, you're good. Use my fear of hospitals against me."

"It's even worse than that," offered Davis, "I have a list of instructions from Dr. Shafer, and, if I'm not mistaken, they are in Colleen's handwriting."

"Orders from high command."

"Exactly! It says right here that I am to give you a dose of pain medicine so that you'll be knocked out for a few hours. The physical therapist will be here later this afternoon and we want you pain-free for the new drill sergeant."

"That stuff makes me silly," confessed Zacharias. "It puts me to sleep for while, but as I'm waking, well the weirdest stuff happens. Did you know that the nurse who took my blood pressure at the hospital can slide under doors without opening them?"

"I doubt it," said Davis.

"Well she denied it, too, but I saw her do it. I told Doc Shafer and she said that I shouldn't believe everything I see. Then again, when the fuzziness leaves, there's no pain."

"Well, they want you alert in two hours and free from pain so that you can jump through their hoops."

"Just don't cross my legs."

"See, you're getting it."

"I sure am!"

Davis poured out a glass of water and gave Burt a single white pill from the amber plastic vial whose label matched the directions on the instruction sheet. Colleen had laid out everything so neatly with her usual efficiency. On the table was a heavy dark walnut post which was counter-weighted to carry a brass ship's bell. It was engraved *S.S. Booker T. Washington.* "Is this an actual bell from your ship?" he asked.

"It's just a toy," said Burt, "the kind you yachtsmen use when you're having cocktails on board. We had a bunch of them made up when we had a crew reunion in 1971."

"Do you have reunions on a regular basis?"

"It wasn't exactly a reunion. It was Captain Mulzac's funeral. Somebody came up with the idea that we should all have ship's bells to ring when we lost another comrade. We ring them twenty-two times. One for each round trip over five years. Carried eighteen thousand troops. They keep trying to say we did it for the money, but nobody got rich and a lot of good men died."

Davis could tell that the medication was having its effect. Zacharias' speech was slowing. McGowan knew that he was on the edge of a longer story, but that he would not hear the ending today.

"Bastards," announced Zacharias, and then his words became incoherent and morphed into snoring.

"Sorry to send you off on such a sour note," said Davis, and suddenly he heard the chime of a bell. He looked at the bell which sat on the buffet, but the sound was from outside. It was the hourly chime of the carillon at St. Luke's just a few blocks away. It rang clear and true.

Colleen had tied a short painter to the clapper on the *Washington* bell. In the note she said that the end of the *line* should be pinned to Burt's pillow so that it could be rung from the bed. Davis smiled at McQuisten's choice of words. He supposed she had been corrected again and again about the use of the word rope and line when referring to ship's cordage. *A rope is a line that hasn't been taken out of the plastic bag yet* was the way McGowan had been taught at the Annapolis Sailing School. Colleen had probably heard something similar, but in the blue-water merchant marine translation.

* * * *

It was nearly two-o'clock when Colleen pulled into the driveway. Davis was getting restless. He had done as much as he could on his laptop, and returned all the calls that needed attention. Burt slept soundly once the initial turbulence had passed. At four-thirty the therapist was scheduled to visit. By then, he would be through the "fuzzy" time of his medication and pain-free. Already he was stirring, but was having a bedside conversation with his son, Hugh, who was not within two hundred miles.

"Well?" said Davis when Colleen had parked the car and came into the house.

"Well, what?" she answered.

"Did you and Rachel find a place?"

"Oh, that," she answered. "We looked at a few apartments. I guess I have sticker shock. You don't get much for $800, do you?"

"That's why we live out in Huron," he said. "Cost of living is lower on my retirement income." As he said the words, he realized that, even in retirement, he probably had more income than she.

"But the commute would kill us. We have one car between us, and it belongs to Burt," she reminded Davis. "How's he doing?"

"Starting to rouse now, just climbing back into sobriety. He's been talking to Hugh."

"Can't blame him for that," she said. "It was nice to have the boys home last weekend. I think that's part of the problem." Davis' expression was her invitation to continue. "I've lived here most of my life. It's hard to think of moving into a couple of rooms with neighbors so close. It must be what old people go through when they go to a nursing home, only that would be even worse."

"They're *retirement* homes now," corrected Davis, "and they go because there are not many other choices. They are forced to scale everything down to a few pieces of familiar furniture and a walker," he added nodding to the aluminum quadruped with puce-colored tennis balls on the front feet which was sitting next to Zacharias' hospital bed.

"Well, he won't have to leave here if I can help it," she said. "Rachel's lease runs through the end of

October, so we don't have to decide anything quite yet. We are still agreed on the plan in principle, it's just…"

"More emotional than you thought," said Davis.

"Yes, it surprised me. Looking at the model unit, just hit me hard."

"Who hit you? I'll scuttle their sorry butt!" Colleen and Davis turned to see Burt sitting up in bed with a sparkle in his eyes.

"Have you been faking sleep while eavesdropping, old man?" asked Davis.

"Have I been asleep? Last I remember I was getting along pretty well with that ambulance driver."

Davis laughed. "He was hitting on her," he said to Colleen. "I think she was ready to give him her phone number." The two joined in the guffaw.

"Well, now his chaperone is back," said Colleen. "How are you feeling, Burt?" she said in an empathetic tone.

"Very glad to be home," he offered without hesitation. "A hospital is no place to be sick. Can't sleep; everybody pokin' places that shouldn't be poked. No, I'm glad to be sprung from that place."

"Well the physical therapist will be here in a hour to teach you some simple exercises to improve your mobility," she said. "And I don't think you should be too grumpy. You want her to come back."

"When have I ever been grumpy to a lady?"

Colleen raised her right hand and unfolded one finger after another as if counting, then her left. "I guess I don't have enough fingers," she confessed.

"Ah, but who's to say that they were ladies?"

"You almost got into trouble with that male chauvinist talk a few hours ago," warned Davis. "I won't cover for you this time. Anyway, you seem alert and rarin' to go, so I'll just run back to the church and see if they have any word on that Thursday workshop that the Presbytery is holding."

"That's right," commented McQuisten, "You're supposed to learn how to be spiritual, I wish we could get Burt there."

"What's that," said Zacharias, "church during the week?"

"He'd set us back years," said Davis, "better keep him tied to that bell. Take care, Burt, you should save your energy for four-thirty. There's going to be a new watch commander.

"Aye, aye," he said.

Davis and Colleen were moving toward the front door. "Is there anything that I need to do on Thursday? For the Reformed Spirituality Conference?"

"No, I think I'm signed up to suffer. Jim Kelly, the presenter is flying in from Stoneypoint, and his flight is arriving at Hopkins at six-thirty in the morning. The exec will pick him up, but they'll be running to get here by eight. He's traveling light, so I don't think they'll be hung up in baggage claim. I told them that I'd have coffee and bagels waiting and we could finalize the room arrangements. The main group will be arriving between eight-thirty and nine. Jenks will have everything set."

"So you'll be there ahead of me? What if I'm a little late?"

"Because of Burt?"

"If everything goes well this afternoon with his initial evaluation, the therapist is going to come back early on Thursday. I could leave the door open for her, but if Burt is still on this medication plan, well..."

"He might be disoriented," said Davis, finishing her sentence.

"Exactly. My hunch is that he's going to be off the pills as soon as he's decided that Dr. Shafer is treating him like an old man who's afraid of a little pain."

"I think you're right. Jenks and I will be there by seven forty-five. The rest of the staff will be there for the event itself. Alistair is going to play the piano at the opening. We should be well represented by eight-thirty or nine."

"Well, if it's up to Burt, I'll be there at my usual time. He doesn't want me to lose any hours, but all of a sudden he doesn't seem as invincible as he used to be."

"At eighty-seven I think he's entitled."

"Thanks."

"For what?"

"For helping with Burt. I know he appreciates it, and I do too."

"It's part of my job description."

"No, it's not. Nobody expects you to sit here for three hours."

"Actually, I got a lot of work done. As far as the church goes, this is one of my days to work out of my home anyway. Just so you know, I used to get in trouble in Dayton for doing things that were supposedly beneath my job classification. In Dayton, I changed light bulbs, rewired a telephone, and played freeze tag at youth club. Everyone should have a hobby!"

"Well, thanks anyway."

* * * *

Nostalgia came upon Davis as he sat in heavy traffic on Detroit Avenue. He had grown up in North Olmsted, but Lakewood had been a part of his early life. South and west of where he inched along was the Civic Auditorium, at the corner of Franklin and Bunts. It was there, through the entrance guarded by a much larger-than-life Johnny Appleseed that he experienced his first live, professional theater production. The play was *Hamlet, Prince of Denmark* and the legion of yellow school buses in the parking lot was the evidence that this was a school field trip. He knew at the time that he would enjoy the time away from class and the innocent shenanigans of the ride, but was doubtful that Mr. Shakespeare would be entertaining. In eighth grade he had suffered through *As You Like It* and preferred anything that was written in English rather than the *fardel* of syllables that the teacher said was greatness. What the hell was a *fardel* anyway, and how can looking up every word in a dictionary be called *reading*? Then Hamlet came out on the stage with intonation and inflection, gestures and fog rising over the parapets. The English was perfect. It was the beginning of Davis' awareness that the sound of words is as important as the letters. This awareness of sound was reinforced over years in the same auditorium, but not always by a professional company.

Davis sang in the high school choir, and the choir always sang at graduation ceremonies that took place in Lakewood rather than the too small assembly areas of North Olmsted. Over the years, the underclassmen would witness the pomp of the ceremony and the giddy adolescence of the out-going seniors. Davis also noted that the Superintendent of Schools had only one speech in his bag of tricks. He knew it was a rerun the second time he heard it in his sophomore year. It wasn't that the content was so memorable, but that the sound of the words was so un-Shakespearian. Davis chuckled in the traffic standstill, remembering the exact phrase that caught his ear. It was part of an illustration about the value of education. An old man tells a traveler to take some pebbles from a streambed. When he pulls them from his pocket later, they are semiprecious stones. It was not the brilliance of the story that McGowan heard, it was the non-musicality of the words. To his young, NE Ohio, Webster's English ear, something that was *semi* precious should sound like the truck that hauled freight. But these stones were *semmie* precious. Later in his education he would hear other regions and nationalities in the voices of his friends. In those early years, accents beyond the Western Reserve sounded alien.

There was a break in the western stream of traffic, so he turned north on Cove and then left onto Clifton Boulevard. From there it was a straight shot past

Edgewater and toward Public Square. He was back to present reality. He thought about the challenges that Burt still faced, and the quiet apprehension that Colleen masked. He had still not heard the longer story of the *Booker T.*, but there'd be time in the weeks ahead. McQuisten was right that this was not a part of his job description, but he liked the old man and the story would be worth hearing in full.

Chapter 24

Cop Killer

McGowan found no surprises at the office on his return. Bob Craig, the retired associate was talking with Donna Adams about recruiting a team of volunteers to serve a dinner at Malachi's soup kitchen and shelter. They hadn't expected Davis on a Tuesday, so they urged him to hit the road and spend an evening with Beth. He didn't need to be persuaded, and set off in time to miss the heaviest of the rush hour. The Indians were on the road so he got on the interstate at the East Ninth Street ramp near the ballpark. It had a corporate name now. In the end, every landmark and building could be converted to advertising, but he still thought of it as "Jake". In an hour, he was turning off Route 2 and into Huron, Ohio.

September is one of those perfect months along the lakeshore. He and Beth walked to the Boat Basin and to Lake Front Park where they sat on a green bench under the long shadow of a ginkgo tree. Three sets of sails, with the sun behind them, were beating toward the lighthouse and their home marina on the Huron River. He recognized the boats, and knew that he was home.

That evening as the eleven o'clock news came on, the phone rang. It had been years since his regular days in the parish, but his stomach tightened with the old response to phones ringing after the hours of politeness.

The caller ID gave the name, *Lynn Samuels*, Huron's mayor. "I wonder what this is about?" thought Davis. He was relieved that it was not one of Beth's sisters calling with bad news.

"Hello," he said.

"Davis, this is Lynn Samuels. I am sorry to call you so late, but I thought you could help. We've had an incident. I don't know if you know Abe Todd or not. He retired from the police force maybe ten years ago. He still helps out some. Anyway, he was working traffic control at a high school scrimmage tonight when a call came through to the regulars who were there. The Sandusky police were in pursuit of someone coming east along Cleveland Road. He shouldn't have done it, but Abe jumped into a patrol car and they went out to try to stop the guy. They blocked off the road by Barnes Nursery, and they pulled the car Abe was in across Camp Road so that he couldn't escape that way.

"From what I've been told, they jumped out of the car, but Todd didn't get away fast enough and the guy took the corner when he saw the main blockade and hit him."

"Where is he now?" asked McGowan.

"He was taken to Sandusky, but they're talking about flying him into Cleveland, University, I think, but maybe the Clinic. That's why I called you. I know that you're working in Cleveland. The family isn't into church, Abe is kinda gruff, but his wife, Ruthie is a sweetie."

She's going to need somebody."

"Is she at the hospital now?"

"I don't know. Ruth's sister was going to drive her to Sandusky, but I don't know if they've left yet."

"I'll try to meet up with her at the hospital here," said McGowan.

"Thanks, Davis," and the call was over.

"Beth, I have to get over to Sandusky Hospital. There's been a bad accident and Lynn Samuels asked me to help."

"You're retired!" quipped Beth.

"Yes, but they're shipping this guy off to Cleveland."

"And that's your turf."

"Apparently so." He grabbed a navy blue sport coat to wear over his Harbor North tee-shirt. Jeans and a jacket would not be appropriate dress at Old First, but he was in Huron. He *had* learned some of the variations in cultural subtleties over the years. Without thinking, he went west out of town on Cleveland Road. He saw flashing lights ahead as he passed Sawmill Creek Resort.

"I shouldn't have come this way," he thought to himself. But the mangled wreckage was toward the railroad crossing on Camp Road and traffic was flowing fine in his direction. Cleveland Road provided a straight shot to Sandusky and the Cedar Point Causeway. This was *Ohio's Vacationland* according to the brochures, but his destination was the Sandusky Regional Medical

Center and this route would take him through a maze of car-lined streets well off the tourist trek.

The parking garage had open spaces on the first level, and Davis was still pocketing his keys by the time he entered the glass corridor that led to the ER. He explained to the attendant behind the security window that he had been sent by Mayor Samuels to support the family of Abe Todd.

He had learned long ago not to claim the title of pastor when visiting people who were not a part of his congregation. He had heard "they don't belong to any church" from well-meaning friends, only to run into another pastor in the hospital room. Then again, hospital staff were aware of the *soul-savers* who injected themselves into the lives of strangers in a moment of crisis. Better to be up-front. He did not know Abe or Ruth; he had been asked by the mayor to make sure that a person important to the town wasn't alone.

Lynn Samuels was accurate in her assessment and the hospital staff was relieved that he was there.

"We are getting ready to transport to University Circle," said the emergency room physician who came out to meet with him. The ID that dangled on a steel clip read *Dr. William Kumar.* He began to explain that Abe had been stabilized, actually, he was on life support and his head injuries did not make the prognosis good.

"I killed a pig! I killed a pig!" came a loudly delighted cry from behind a yellow drawn curtain. Two uniformed police simultaneously jumped toward the sound.

"Careful," cried Kumar after them. "He has a broken arm."

"If he doesn't shut up, he'll have a broken mouth," said a deeper voice behind the drape.

"We'll move him out of here," said the doc. "Is there an open consultation room?" he said, turning to a nurse.

"Right away," he said, "I'll get him moved." The male nurse yanked back the fabric screen. The two cops were in the face of the skinny kid who had a wriggling tattooed snake where eyebrows used to be.

"You can't touch me." He whimpered, "I know my rights!"

"He's so high, he wouldn't feel it anyway," said Kumar interceding for the kid who was registering high on the officers' punk scale.

"Just so you know," said one of the uniformed men as he drew up close enough to bite the snake. "You didn't kill a pig. You hit an old man. You hit a grandpa. If that's going to be your claim to fame, you are even more pathetic than you look!"

Davis could tell that the staff was rushing now to lower the decibels and defuse an explosion. He could not blame the police. Their rage was raw and real, but the book says *if you lose control, the creep will walk.*

Davis knew about suppressing emotion for the sake of duty. Even now he wanted to shout Beth's words as a mantra, "I'm retired," but he had returned to this life of standing with people who had lost the ability to stand up for themselves. Right now, the person's name was Abe Todd and he was a grandfather. He wondered if there was anyone to stand with the cop killer, maybe a mother whose heart was shattered as badly as Todd's skull, or a father whose frustration would be as hot as the cops at the bedside. Then again, maybe *the creep* didn't even have that.

After the patient was sequestered in a small room, Kumar returned. "Sorry about that," he said as if it were routine. "He wasn't hurt badly, but he was drugged up before they brought him in. We've given him Xanax; he should come down to earth."

"Doctor," a middle-aged woman in blues approached. "Mr. Todd's wife is on her way. Do you want us to take her in to see him?"

Kumar looked at McGowan. "Are you willing to go in with her, Reverend?"

"Yes," said Davis. "I'll want to talk with her first."

"Of course. Excuse us, we need to clean things up a bit." As they moved away, one of the officers approached McGowan.

"I didn't know you were a Reverend," he said. "I'm sorry about my behavior out here."

"You're human," said Davis, blowing off the comment.

"He shouldn't have been there. He was only helping direct the parking at the high school."

"I know a little of what happened," said Davis, "but Ruth is on her way in and it would be good to have more answers."

"We got the call. This guy was coming down Cleveland Road, really barreling. We were going to throw out spike strips in the hope he'd go into one of the fields before he hit Rye Beach Road and all the congestion in that area. Abe jumped into my car, and I didn't have time to argue.

"The guy was really moving, and there was no way we were going to set up between Perkins and Camp Road, so we set up across from Sheldon Marsh. The preserve is on one side and an empty lot is on the other. I was supposed to pass through before they set the strips and park across Camp Road so he'd be funneled into the right place. We got there. I stopped the engine, and told Abie to move it. We had to get clear of the car..."

"And he didn't," added Davis to fill the silence.

"No, he didn't. He's an old man. In his sixties, I'd guess. Not as fast as he used to be. Eats too much of Ruthie's cooking. Don't tell her that."

"I won't," said McGowan. The name on the silver name-bar said *Cameron*, but Davis didn't know how to address this young man who had the misguided notion that a man in his sixties was automatically *old*. "What's your name?"

"Curt, Curtis Cameron," said the cop.

"Curt, he chose to get into the car. He understood the risks."

"I know. I told him that he shouldn't be running on a call. He said, 'Are you going to jabber or drive?' So I drove. When I stopped, I just told him to run like hell. We knew from the chatter that it was just seconds."

"And he wasn't fast enough."

"I once saw a deer get hit on the Interstate. That thing flew straight up. All I can see right now is Abe blasted into the dark. You know the high grass there by the railroad tracks? He was thrown pretty far and it was dark. We got snake eyes controlled and then we started looking. It took us half an hour to find him. I thought he was dead, but the squad worked on him and brought him here. He's broken pretty bad."

"Well they got him here alive." Davis knew enough about head injuries to know that the vital signs on the ER machines were not always good predictors of whether or not a person's life had been saved. Curt Cameron knew that too.

"Would you help me talk to Ruth when she gets here?" Davis asked.

"I don't know if I could tell her all that…"

"You don't have to. This isn't the time anyway. I think she will find it comforting to know that you were with him and the guys found him and did all that they could. Your just being here will say that without any words."

The decision to stay or not was preempted by Dr. Kumar who was directing a stocky woman in a faded black *Dale Earnhart* sweatshirt and jeans. "Reverend, this is Ruth Todd."

Her eyes went to Davis and then quickly to Cameron. "Hello, Ruthie," said the cop. She rushed to him and threw her arms around him. "I'm sorry," he said, "he shouldn't have been there."

"Oh, you couldn't stop him," she said. "How did it happen?"

Cameron's eyes told Davis that he was not ready to talk. "Curt had just pulled across the lanes to block the road. He and Abe were trying to get away from the vehicle when the guy came around the corner and hit him." Ruth heard the words from Davis and then looked back at Cameron for confirmation.

"That's what happened," he said. "Abie didn't have a chance. Never saw what hit him."

"I can only give you a few minutes," said the physician, "we're ready to transport him. The chopper is on the pad."

"Can I see him then?" asked Ruth.

"Briefly. The next seventy-two hours are critical. We've given him medicine to put him in a coma. He won't be able to talk with you. He's on a ventilator."

"Can I come with him to the hospital?" she asked.

"No," he said, "there is not room in the helicopter. Every bit of space is needed for the life-support equipment. Your husband is very critical."

"But you said he has been stabilized," she said.

"Yes," he answered in a clinical tone. "The support equipment is maintaining him so that we can get him to the hospital in Cleveland. He has many hours of surgery tonight and they are getting ready to receive him. For your sake, I would see him now and go home until tomorrow. Everyone is doing their best."

"I think I should go with him."

"You will only tire yourself needlessly," Kumar insisted. "They will keep him in a coma. If he recovers, he will need your company for many weeks. You must prepare for that eventuality. Believe me, everyone is doing our best. Your husband is a police officer, and he will be accorded respect."

McGowan heard the little words *if* and *coma.* Of course they would induce coma with head injuries to guard against brain swelling, but they often reversed the drug regimen to see if there was any responsiveness. He had to wonder what level of brain function was left. Or was there a certain protocol of correctness that had to be honored with a person injured in the line of duty. Were all these heroics simply insurance against the possibility that a defense lawyer would try to argue that the death was not the result of a client's actions but of lack of aggressiveness on the part of the medical team? Was that the *respect* that Abie would be accorded? For the sake of justice, he would be kept clinically alive until there could be no further argument. It was the price cops pay. Curt had to fight to control his natural rage, and Abe, without a choice, had to fight to win back the life of a vegetable. Meanwhile Ruthie watched.

"I think the doctor is right," agreed Davis. "I'm sure that the hospital there will give you a phone number so that you can call directly to his nurse at any time."

"Certainly," said Kumar, who nodded to the assistant by his side. She took the meaning and went to get the number for the intensive care unit.

"In the morning, your family can gather at the hospital in Cleveland. I will be there, too and I'm sure you'll be able to see him then."

"I'll drive, if you like," offered Cameron.

"But don't you have to work?" she protested, then changer her mind, "I'd like that. It would make Abe proud."

McGowan saw that Kumar was getting antsy. "Maybe we should go in now," Davis said. "Just remember that he won't look like himself. There will be a lot of tubes and wires, but that's not him. He can't see himself. If he can hear you just a little, it'll be your voice tone that tells him how you are feeling. I know it's a big job, but try to sound as natural as you can."

They walked to the end of the room where the nurse drew back the curtain. In his retirement, Davis had forgotten the shock of the sight that was second nature to hospital workers. Abe Todd lay stretched out on an elevated slab of a table, his swollen face protruding from gauze bindings on the right side of his skull, a hint of red leaching through the packing. His eyes were taped shut against drying, a clear tube down his throat, and the steady click-click hiss of the forced breathing. He was naked except for adhesive leads attached to his chest, front and side. He was a big man, but his girth was magnified by swelling tissue that stretched his skin and made his fingers look like sausages.

"Hello, Abe. I'm Davis McGowan. Mayor Samuels asked me to come check on you. She wanted you to know that everyone is pulling for you, we're thinking about you and praying. Ruth is here."

The big man twitched at the words. Davis did not know if it was an involuntary reaction to a cool draft from the curtain being opened or a response to the words. At this point, it made little difference. He understood it as a gift to Ruth.

"He knows you're here," said Davis who knew nothing for certain.

"Abie, Honey, it's Ruth. They're taking really good care of you. We can't stay, but we will be with you tomorrow when you get settled." She fought back both her tears and her shock at the sight. The paraphernalia put her off and she pulled back. Davis reached over and took Abe's right hand that was held secure at his side with canvas strips.

"We don't have much time," he said. "Would you like me to say a prayer?"

"Please," she said, losing the sound of the word in a whisper. Davis stepped to the side, and she reached out to touch her husband.

"It's okay," assured McGowan. After a brief prayer, the three were led back out into the corridor and a flurry broke out around Abie's bed while practiced hands disconnected and reconnected the life support to the more portable units that would keep the cop alive for the ride of his life.

Further down the hall, Davis saw the second uniformed officer seated next to a closed door. He jumped to his feet when Ruth emerged from the ER. He held his post. McGowan was not sure whether he was at a loss as to what he should say to Ruth Todd, or whether his duty held him. No sound came from the room behind him, but Davis knew it was holding a man who hoped to be a cop killer.

Chapter 25

Fear of Woz

To everyone else it had to look like a normal Tuesday, but Richard Kosten couldn't help but feel a growing excitement about the week. On Thursday, he would speak with Rachael. By the luck of the calendar the 10th fell on a Thursday, so his first words of address would be at her house rather than on the No. 55 bus. There was a certain auspiciousness that came with such an alignment of the universe. The only real unknown was waving at him from behind the sliding glass doors.

Heather had told him about a Lakewood cop who asked questions about his protective shoe coverings. She had not betrayed him, but she represented a risk that had to be considered. She kept silent when the plain-clothed man asked Wozniak the question. Richard wondered what she would have done had the question been addressed to her. It was not, but he also suspected that her dislike of her supervisor had more to do with her silence than her loyalty to him. What if she were to let go of her secret in the midst of a verbal spar? He had been in family fights where secret words pour out, and once voiced, impossible to rebottle.

He finished his cigarette and stepped out of the white van. He was not going to jog Wozniak's memory by wearing surgical booties. Instead, he had a new pair of shoes with light colored soles.

"Nice shoes!" said Heather leaning against the frame of the open door like a pole dancer he had seen in a club. He always thought she was hot, and she was always flirty.

"You seem happy tonight," he said ignoring the reference to footwear. "Did Mr. Wozniak call in sick?"

"No, the *Wizard of Woz* is still here and still clueless."

Kosten wasn't sure how to understand the comment. Was it a general rebuff of her boss or a reference to his own work habits?

"I'm just happy because I don't have to put up with him much longer. He doesn't know it yet, but tomorrow is my last day."

"You're moving on? What about us?"

"Dickybird, there's no us. You missed your chance last weekend."

"Last weekend?"

"I'm surprised you didn't hear the explosion. Saturday night I had to work 'til close and my drawer was the last one pulled, so I had to deal with Mr. Wozniak. I was pretty pissed when I left, so I stopped at my husband's favorite watering hole on Detroit. His truck was in the lot, so I went in to let him pick me up."

"And he wasn't there," interrupted Kosten.

"Better for him if he wasn't," responded Heather. "He was dancing with his hand on the butt of some red-headed skank with a bad dye job. You should have seen him jump when I smacked the Wicked Witch of the West."

Are you living in the Wizard of Oz? thought Kosten, but he said, "You actually popped her?"

"Actually, I didn't touch her. I just smacked Romeo's hand hard enough to leave fingerprints. They both got the message and he didn't get any all weekend."

"Guess I did miss my chance to stand in."

"I spent the evening dancing with every guy there. He had to watch from where I made him sit in the corner."

"What about the skank?"

"She got her sorry ass out of there, and I got offered a job waiting tables on the weekends. I can make more in tips in two nights than a twenty-four hour week here. That's all they want to give me. He wants to drink with his buddies and throw darts; he can do it where I can keep an eye on his roving hands."

"Meanwhile, every drunk in the room will be trying to get into your pants."

"I can have any guy I want, and he knows it. I think it kinda turns him on; we'll see."

"Where is this bar? Maybe I'll come to take a try."

"Oh, but you'd be my weakness, Dickybird. You're too pretty to let him see. I'll have to keep you my secret! Anyway, tomorrow night, at closing I am going to give Mr. Wozniak my own version of *his* performance review. I'll start with the category of *asshole*, that's the one where he *exceeds expectations*."

"Sorry that it's not my night to do the floors," he responded. "Sounds like it could be quite a show. Don't you have to give two weeks' notice?"

"I don't give a damn about a reference from him. He wouldn't give me a good one if I was Snow White." Richard wondered if she'd ever read a book or watched anything but old movies and Disney cartoons.

"I'll wait until *after* I punch out," she continued. "I'll rant on my own time, and I'll bet anything that my name will just fall off the schedule for the next two weeks. I'll take Thursday night off, and then play for tips from the bad boys on Friday."

"Sounds like a plan," said Richard. "It might be smarter to go quietly, though."

"And that's the difference between us, Dickybird. You always play it safe. You should have moved on me a year ago. Sometimes you just have to take a ride on the wild side. Maybe you should come over and I'll give you a lesson."

"Maybe I will," he said.

"Do you like the way the world looks when you're down on the floor scraping gum and erasing heel marks in your little blue booties?" Kosten felt himself flushing.

"Don't worry, I won't out you to the Wizard," she said. "Why is that cop looking for you? Do they need someone to wax the floors in the precinct restrooms?" She laughed as though she had heard the best joke ever. Richard tightened his gut as if waiting for a punch by his mother, but none came. The attack was only verbal. All he could hear was *Keep walking, you're too big to carry!* It was a portion of the monologue he first heard when he was three. He had been at Edgewater Park with his parents. They were fighting, again. His father had choked his mother, then broke his hold when he saw Dicky looking at him curiously. *Was this what happened at night when he was awakened in his crib by noises from the other room?*

They were stranded near the lake when his father drove off with the car and he and his mother had to walk back to their apartment in Lakewood. "He's gone now, because of you," she had said. "He'll never come back. You saw him, he wants me dead. That'll be the only thing that will make *him* happy."

"Well, it sounds like you've made your mind up," said Richard with a cool calmness in his voice. Thursday was precious to him. She would not jeopardize it in an adolescent rant against an EXA. He had less than twenty-four hours, but he was cleverer than she could ever guess.

Chapter 26

Dead End

Darnell hated to admit to himself that he and Megan had not been able to track down anything to mitigate the likelihood that a Lakewood citizen would be dead on Thursday. Now he had to admit it to his commander, Boyd Wakeman. When he opened the door to Wakeman's office, he was pleased to see Megan sitting on one of the black vinyl upholstered chairs in front of the steel-gray desk. She looked at him and smiled.

"Come in, Wilson. Sorento has been telling me that every lead has been a dead end."

"So far," admitted Darnell.

"The time is running out fast, but it was a long-shot from the beginning. I've shared my concerns with Cleveland, and they've agreed to put more people on the ground at Edgewater tomorrow. They have camera surveillance, but if this guy is out there, I'd like to preempt this year's murder."

"I think I should go back to Wallace's and talk to more people," blurted Wilson. "The assistant manager wasn't much help with identifying outside vendors who use shoe coverings when they are in the store, but it was late at night, and he was getting ready to close. Probably had a lot on his mind."

"If it's the best you have, sure, why not. Still, we're a long way from a name or a description. If Cleveland picks up the guy tomorrow, it might help the Prosecutor build a case. I'd rather have something, anything to give out at a briefing."

"Boyd, I'd like to go with Darnell," said Sorento.

"Good idea. Another set of eyes and ears might help."

Wilson had to shake off the exuberance that rode on the anticipation of spending a few bonus hours with Megan. *This is business*, he kept thinking to himself. He knew that for today at least, he would be with Agent Sorento and they would maintain focus. His suspicion was confirmed as they left the building and headed out toward the parking lot.

"I think maybe I should talk with the people at the registers," she said. "They probably pay more attention to what's happening on the floor than the managers," she said.

"Thanks for seeing me through with this, Agent Sorento," he said.

"Always glad to help my favorite cop," she offered. "After tomorrow, we can be different. One way or the other."

"It would be nice to break this one," he added.

"Better than a box of chocolates."

Chapter 27

Hearing Goes Last

It took Davis while to find Abie Todd's family. They had sequestered themselves in the corner of the waiting room. Ruth was sheltered from view by two large men, Abe's sons, if the genetic markers and body-type were to be trusted.

"This is Dan, and this is Ben," said Ruth introducing the pair. They both must have been in their mid-forties, but they looked as if they were dressed out of different decades. Dan wore khaki Dockers and a scarlet and gray OSU polo shirt. Ben looked as though he had pulled his clothes out of the laundry hamper of a heavy-metal groupie. Ben was fidgeting as if the nicotine was failing him.

"Have you been in to see him yet?" asked McGowan.

"They say it will be a few minutes They've been saying that for an hour," said Ruth. "The nurse was just out."

Dan appeared stoic, but Ben inflated his cheeks and made a hard blow as if trying to expel all his inner demons in a single blast. "I don't know if I can do this," he said.

"Do what?" asked McGowan.

"See the old bastard, lying out there like a piece of meat."

His choice of words confused Davis. He had known men whose use of words like *fuckin'*, *bastard*, and *son of a bitch*, were simply the *um's* and *ah's* that fell between the syllables of the real words. Some used the words to endear, like the young mother who kept referring to her newborn as a *little rat fink*. He had wondered what ever happened when the little boy found out what the words really meant.

"Ben, he's your father," said Ruthie, and Davis knew that the words were raw emotion, not patterns of speech.

"We've only fought these last ten years," said Ben. "He wouldn't let up."

"Who wouldn't let up?" quipped Dan.

"That's the way he is," said their mother, "he just wanted to keep you both in line and do the right thing." The silence that followed told Davis that this conversation had played out many times before and would not be resolved now.

"We're ready now," said a woman in yellow scrubs and a dangling mask hanging from her throat like a blue seashell. They followed through the swinging door into a corridor lined with sinks and piles of hospital gowns.

"I am going to ask you to scrub your hands and put on a gown and shoe coverings." With that, she disappeared around the corner leaving the trio in confusion.

"Here," said Davis as he pushed to get a handful of soap from the dispenser. He had learned how to wash his hands for surgery when he was in high school and worked as an orderly at Fairview General. He used his right elbow to operate the flat paddles on the cold and hot spigots. "They want to protect him from any germs we might be carrying in on our hands and clothes," he said. "He's probably too weak now to fight off even simple infections."

Davis knew that he was only telling part of the truth, but it would help them make sense of the strange world that they were about to enter. When the nurse returned, she announced her approval and led them all to the crypt where Abe Todd was laid out.

McGowan noted that the bed was still raised at an operating room level. The massive bandages of the head were much reduced, but it was obvious that the head beneath them was no longer round.

"He's still in a coma," she began. "That's to be expected. It keeps him still and not fighting the ventilator. He will not be able to talk, but he might know you are here."

The four stood in a line facing the side of the bed for a long time, but only fifty seconds by the clock. Dan took his mother's arm and stepped back away from the bedside.

Davis looked around. The room seemed odd in that it was so large. He was used to ICU pods with tight spaces crisscrossed with tubes and wires. Here there were open areas where machines could be rolled in or had been rolled out after the heroics had run their full course. Some of the read-outs on the machines were obvious, breathing rate and volume, blood gases, pulse EKG. The EEG looked almost flat, but McGowan didn't want to speculate. It could have been something as simple as a loose connection or the depth of the drug-induced coma. Ben was sobbing quietly. Davis edged toward his side.

"I didn't hate him," said the young man. "I just could never please him and got tired of trying."

"Did you ever tell him that?" asked McGowan.

"We shouted more than we ever talked."

"If it's like your mother said, at one time he thought getting on your back would help you."

"He always wanted me to be like Dan, and I couldn't be. He was always older and stronger. He was always first-string and I was in the meatballs. I didn't care."

"Sounds like you did."

"I wish I could have told him that I didn't like fighting him."

"Tell him now."

"He can't hear."

"You don't know that. The nurse said he couldn't talk. One thing I've learned over the years is that you can't tell what people can hear when they are in a coma. I've had conversations at beds like this and two days later, after the guy comes to, he tells me what I said. The hearing is the last thing to go. He might be hearing everything you're saying now."

"But I can't talk to him now."

"Why not? It may be the best chance you'll ever get."

"Dad..." Davis backed away from the area and joined Ruth and Dan. Words were being spoken behind him, but they were not meant for his hearing.

"Thank you for coming, Rev. McGowan," said Ruth. "Ben and Abie have had some rough times lately. It wasn't always that way; it's going to be hard on him."

Dan and Ruth rejoined Ben at the bedside. Ruth asked Davis for a prayer like he had offered the night before. "Abie wasn't big on churches," she said, "but I think it's important."

The visit was over, and the yellow scrub suit returned. Davis was pleased that the two men took their mother's arms as she walked between them. He followed behind and when they disappeared through the door to the waiting area, he turned to speak with the attendant.

"I'm their minister," he said, "What are they facing?"

"You'd have to talk with the doctor," she said.

"I don't need test results to see how serious this is," he said. "Do I encourage them to stay or pace themselves for a long slog?"

"I don't think it will be long," she said. "His heart is strong, but the only real brain activity there is in the stem. The ventilator is assisting his breathing, but that's all involuntary. Whether he's still there, I can't say."

"Thank you," said Davis.

* * * *

The trip in from University Circle didn't seem as long as the ride out. He took the Euclid Corridor, a route that he had avoided in favor of Chester during the orange barrel days of its reconstruction. Businesses were coming back, and Playhouse Square seemed to be anchoring the recovery.

Activity at Old First was in high gear. Years ago, Davis concluded that the program year had to be planned in the summer, because once Labor Day came, it was all autopilot until Pentecost. Alistair Montgomery was working with Colleen editing a draft of his music brochure which advertised the annual *Brown Bag Concert Series*. A note in his mail slot told him that the final count for the Presbytery's workshop on Reformed Spirituality was forty-two. As pastor of the host church, the number was simply an indicator of how much coffee, how many donuts, and how many lunches would need to be ready, beginning with name badges and open doors at 8:30 a.m. Most of that burden fell to others. Davis simply had to get his butt in gear early enough to beat the morning rush hour. If events at the hospital crashed, all bets were off.

"I need a plan B," said Davis to no one. Bob Craig, the associate emeritus would be a gracious stand-in, but at ninety-two he relied on his daughter to chauffer him. Sarah Adams had taken the week to get her daughter situated at Hanover College in southern Indiana. Colleen had already explained that she would be late because Burt had to be monitored during the fuzzy period of his pain medication in advance of the physical therapist's arrival. Then again, Mark Twain had once observed that the worst things in his life never actually happened. Abie Todd's condition could hold steady for days.

Chapter 28

Vacation

When Bruce McClelland approved two vacation days for Megan Sorento, it neatly purged some of the mounting hours of comp time that she had accumulated. He was not aware, however, that the time she would spend with Darnell Wilson would be following a rabbit trail that had long ago grown cold.

"Maybe I've concocted this conspiracy in my head," said Wilson as they drove toward the pharmacy. "We really don't have any proof that a single killer committed these murders."

"Why are you second guessing?" asked Megan. "All you have is circumstantial, so of course you don't know. But the circumstances are beyond what I would call random. You have three unsolved murders of women from your jurisdiction. Their bodies get dumped across the city line in the same place. Same profile, same dates on a three-year cycle. That's the only thing that seems odd to me. Why three years? The guy is highly organized. Yes, it's circumstantial, but reasonable. He doesn't seem to be opportunistic. He selects these victims to satisfy some drama that's playing out in his head. I suspect that he's getting some power charge from it and it's only a matter of time before he gets more regular in these attacks."

"Maybe he already is," said Darnell. "What if we think these three are the only ones because they are so obvious? Maybe they're the only ones we've been able to find."

"That could be, but the fact is that they *are* so obvious. He wants the bodies found in that place on that date."

"You mean, he wants to be caught?"

"More likely, he's trying to communicate. He's sending a message to someone, acting out the same drama over and over. It's real to him, but only to him."

"And not so real that the department can waste any resources to try an unravel it."

"That's not true, exactly. Boyd has convinced Cleveland to put more personnel at Edgewater tomorrow. While you and I are following a trail of breadcrumbs, the rest of them are betting that a sociopath is going to meet them tomorrow at the rendezvous point."

"So what do we ask at Wallace's?"

"Same questions that you have asked before: Does anyone ever go behind the pharmacy counter besides regular staff? Are there ever people in the store, outside contractors, maybe, who cover their shoes while they are working in the store?"

"Yep," said Darnell, "same questions."

"But a different time of day, and maybe different people to give answers," said Sorento.

"We are quite a pair, aren't we? We both know that the odds are with the patrols at Edgewater, not with us."

"But we're running against the odds," added Megan. "You're right, though. We are quite a pair."

Chapter 29

Short Break

As much as she liked the idea of telling off her supervisor, Heather felt queasy when she thought of actually telling Mr. Wozniak off. It was part of her game plan, and it played out well in her imagination of "I'll say *this*, and he'll say *that*, and I'll zap him by saying *such and such*." She had been through these mind games before and never had she actually been able to retort with *such and such*. These revenge dramas never worked out as imagined.

"Maybe, I should just play sweet," she considered, but that felt less likely than the other. She was coming up on a break, however, and the nicotine would calm her. She walked toward the front of the store and the door slid away at the snap of her fingers. "Did anyone see that?" That was a part of her attitude that *the Woz* couldn't abide. If she could get a rise out of him, it would make checking out so much easier. He didn't see anything, unless it was from one of the surveillance cameras.

Outside, the stars were obscured by the city lights on an otherwise clear night. She turned right, walking along the brick exterior toward the back of the building and away from the main entrance.

"Heather!" she heard a voice from the corner of the lot.

"Dickybird?" She could make out the shape of the young man, but the giveaway was the white van parked just off the premises.

"Thought you might like a last day party," he called hanging back out of the glare of the security light.

"Aren't you a sweetie," she said moving in his direction. "This isn't even your night to be working."

"Thought you could use some moral support," he said, "before you face off with the Wizard."

She looked back at the building where customers were exercising the electric eye on the door. "I just have a few minutes," she said.

"Cigarette, beer, and good company, that's what I can offer; it'll only take a few minutes and you'll be back to your dream job."

"Dream? What have you been smoking?"

"Only tobacco, I swear," he said laughingly. "What will they do, fire you?"

"Good point." By now she was in full smoke mode, and he was pulling open the passenger side door. The dome light surprised him, and he quickly turned his face away from the direction of the store. "Oh, Richard, you take me to all the nicest places," she said mockingly.

"But the company is good," he said jumping quickly into the driver's side seat and closing the door. "Are you going to do it?" he asked.

"If I don't lose my nerve."

"Maybe this will help," he said as he magically produced two beers. He twisted the cap of the first and handed it to her while he struggled with the second.

"I can't have beer breath," she protested.

"And you won't," he said extending a fistful of red swirled peppermints in cellophane wrappers.

"You think of everything," she said, leaning across and kissing him on the cheek.

"I do," he agreed. "If you just drink one, it'll probably be out of your system by the time you're scheduled to go home."

She thought about it, and it made sense. The glass bottle was cold and wet beneath her grip.

"Here's to a new job," he said, raising his bottle in a toast. She mirrored the gesture and took a swig.

"That black cop came back today," she said. "Had a pretty woman with him this time."

"What did he say?" asked Kosten, trying to sound only curious.

"I wasn't here. He came in before my shift, but April said he was cute."

"Did she talk to him?"

"No, the Chick talked to her. Asked about booties and outside people who come in to stock the shelves. April's new; don't think she's ever even been here on a night when you were in doing the floors. She told him about the chip guy and the guys who stock all the pop."

"Was she a cop?"

"Don't think so. He's the one who talked to the manager and showed a badge."

"But she was asking questions?"

"They both were. He wanted to know who else was *ever* allowed back in the pharmacy. 'No one,' she told them. Only people allowed back there are the pharmacists, the techs, and the managers who are supposed to get enough pharmacy training to fill in for a tech if there's an emergency. You know how strict they are about that sort of thing."

Kosten did know, but he also knew that he had been back there once. It was nothing criminal. The pharmacist was there the whole time. In fact, she had invited him. She had been having problems with a technician who was disrespectful to customers. Apparently, the tech also had a habit of depositing her chewing gum on the underside of the counter. Once discovered, the dismissal was put under the category of *just cause*, and Richard was invited in with his scraper to clean the underside of a shelf rather than the polished side of the floor. That was a long time ago, however, and out of the memory of the current staff.

Heather had not realized that he had zoned out on her. She was still reporting, "I guess people go back to change water filters or work on the computers when something goes weird with them." Her words were getting longer and then she couldn't remember exactly what she had been saying.

"How 'bout a fresher brew?" he said and handed her another without bothering to pretend that he was twisting off the cap.

"I have to get back to the store."

"How long is your break?" he asked.

"Fifteen minutes," she said.

"It's only been five, seven at the max," he lied, mostly to gauge the effect of the drug on her sense of time.

"Oh," she said as she took the second beer. This one was a bit warmer but she didn't notice.

On the street the drug was called *purple rain* even though some versions of the pill were not color-matched to the slang. It was a prescription equivalent to a date-rape drug and its prevalence had young women dancing in bars and clubs with drinks in hand. A bottle left alone at the table was drop point for any version of alprazolam. It had been in his mother's medicine cache. She had died two years earlier, and he was counting on the fact that the old medication had not lost any of its potency. Even then, he recognized the anti-anxiety medication and knew that the 1 mg. tablet had other uses. Heather was now on her second dose, and holding tight to the bottle as if it were the only secure point in an otherwise whirling universe.

He reached for the ignition and turned the key. He did not want to face the Woz or anyone else who might come looking for a wayward employee.

"I have to finish my shift," she said, "I haven't even told the jerk that I'm through."

"I am so glad you talked me into staying," he said. "You looked like the cat that swallowed the canary when you walked out after your shift."

"I did?"

"Man, I wish I could have seen the bird's face when you told him. What did he say?"

She searched her brain for a memory and settled on the encounter that she had so graphically imagined. "I told him that he should treat people better, that I wasn't dumb *or* lazy. I knew better than him about who was in and out of the store. Where are we going?"

"Back to my place, don't you remember? We'll call your husband and he can join us there."

"Where's my cell; did I leave it in the store?" She was getting panicky.

"No, it's in the back with the rest of your stuff. We'll call when we get to the apartment."

"He's probably dancing with some skanky bitch anyway."

"Hey, if he doesn't want to come to your last night farewell party, then he's an idiot. I made some jello-shots and we can have a blast. You can crash at my place and let him stay up all night wondering who is patting your fine ass."

"Dickybird, you are so bad, and I think I am sooo drunk."

"You can't be. You just had two beers. It's just the euphoria of smacking down the Wizard of Woz."

"*I'm off to pee on the Wizard...*" She started to sing her own version of the traveling song of Dorothy, Lion, Scarecrow, and Tin Man.

"I think you just found the field of poppies," said Kosten. She was no longer listening, however, and his only concern was that she not be so out of it that she couldn't get up the back stairway.

His concern was not unfounded, but in spite of her rubber legs, they managed. He only had to drag her the last twenty feet and that was from the hallway, through the bedroom, and into his private room behind the wall.

"Heather," he said firmly as he leaned close to her ear. She struggled to mumble something intelligible. Her eyes rolled beneath the lids, but did not open. He stood above her and a wave of pleasure washed over him. She was completely at his mercy, and not a Rachael. She even liked him. Still, she was a distraction and there would be time later. He could keep her medicated until after the more pressing task was complete, and could play after the work was done. Anticipation was part of the seduction. "Let's get this off," he said to her as he pulled away her smock and then the tight fitting black tee beneath it.

She mumbled to somebody in the netherworld, but did not resist.

Chapter 30

Perfect Night

Beth and Davis sat on their screened porch and listened to the last of the cicadae in heat. September was a perfect time in the lakefront town. Traffic through town diminished as tourists were sequestered in their more urban school districts. The ringing phone reminded McGowan that he was only retired in theory, not practice.

"Who would call at ten o'clock?" asked Beth. Davis knew several potential answers to her question even before he saw the readout on the caller ID. It said, *A. Todd* and had the familiar 433 of the Huron exchange.

"It's Ruth Todd," he said, picking up the phone. He was wrong; the voice at the other end was a man.

"Rev. McGowan, this is Dan Todd. I'm sorry to call so late but I just got off the phone with the hospital. They're saying that it's clear that the machines are keeping him alive. No, that's not right. The machines are maintaining his vital signs. They're pretty sure he's dead, but we have to agree to pull the plug."

"How'd your mother take it?"

"She saw it coming, but it's real hard. Dr. Tom gave her something to help her sleep. She'd already taken it before we got the call. She cried for a while, but then fell asleep. I asked them when it had to be done. They said they could hold off for a short time if we wanted to be there. I think we should, don't you?"

"I think that's something Ruth has to decide."

"She says that she's stood by him all these years, and now's no time to quit."

"Then that's the right thing to do," said Davis.

"We asked if they could wait until tomorrow morning, and they said they would. We are going to be there at 8:30. I know it's late, but it would mean a lot to Mom, to all of us, if you could be there, too."

How come it's always like this? thought Davis, *more hoops to jump through!* But what he said was "I'll be there."

He walked back to the porch where the lights were dimmed to confound moths in search of luminous ecstasy. "Beth, would you be willing to sit with Burt tomorrow morning?"

"Was that Colleen on the phone?"

"No, it was Dan Todd. They're disconnecting Abie from life support in the morning. Colleen has already made arrangements to come in late because she has to coordinate Burt's medication before the physical therapist gets there. I have the Presbytery coming in for the spirituality workshop."

"I forgot about that," said Beth. "Of course, I'll do it. What time?"

"Well, I'd like to get to the hospital before the family gets there to see what the arrangements are. The speaker is to arrive around 8:00. If we pick Colleen up a little after 7:00, she'll have time to tell you what to expect. We'll have to leave here by 6:00."

"Ouch! Guess I'd better wash my hair tonight!"

"If you do, just be aware that Burt is going to hit on you."

"Well, he's kinda cute. Are you jealous?" Their chuckle was followed with a kiss and another late-night call to Colleen McQuisten.

"Colleen, this is Davis. I got a call from that family that I visited at University today. We have to rearrange the morning."

Chapter 31

Neighborhood Policing

It was 11:30 when Darnell Wilson's cell went off. He had a simple ring tone that mimicked a land-line phone. It was a no-nonsense feature that fit his professional attitude. When on the job, it did not draw excess attention, at 11:30 with heavy eyes and an ominous day ahead, it made his heart jump. He and Megan had said goodnight two hours earlier, and he doubted if this would be good news.

The call was from a cop in the Second Ward. The neighborhood patrol officer was having a long day, too. He was called to the Wallace Pharmacy just after closing. A clerk had not come back from a break. At first, it was just viewed as an annoying prank, but when the store closed at 10:00, she had still not appeared and her register drawer was left unattended.

The assistant manager had attempted to call her husband. Failing to make contact, he called the Second Ward's neighborhood cop whose job it was to make connections with the people and businesses in the area. While they were getting ready to review the most recent surveillance video, the officer saw Wilson's business card lying on the desktop.

"I thought I'd just give you a heads-up, Darnell," she said.

"This late at night? Thanks, I guess," he said in his best wise-guy voice. "No, I'm kidding; what have you found?"

"It's pretty clear that she just left on her own, but from the fact that she left all her personal stuff behind her cell phone, wallet so, I think she must've intended to come back."

"What do you mean that she 'left on her own'?"

"You can see it on the tape. She walks along the building, lighting up, and then she turns out like someone called to her. The camera at the back of the store got another angle, and it looks like she's reacting to someone just off the premises who's standing next to a light colored van."

"Can you make out who it is?"

"The lighting wasn't good, but there's no struggle to be seen. She got into the van with him and they sat there awhile. The assistant manager, Mr. Wozniak–you've talked with him before–he has the impression that it's a fellow named Richard. He cleans the floors here. The image isn't clear, but he drives a van and has a similar build."

"Can you get a plate number?"

"No, the landscaping shields out the front end. Mr. Wozniak says they were always buddy-buddy when he was on the job."

"Is he there? Can I talk to him?" Darnell heard a muffled he *wants to speak with you* as the phone switched hands.

"Hello," said Wozniak.

"Do you have a last name and address for this guy?"

"No, he's not one of our employees. He works for a janitorial service. They clean a lot of offices and buildings during after-business hours."

"You must have a contact person or emergency number?"

"Yes. I'll have to look it up. The company is Kwik Klean. They are out of Ohio City. They have the cleaning contract with all the stores in this district, so we don't deal with them directly. You can't think that there's anything criminal going on here."

"Why do you say that?" asked Wilson.

"Well, it's just that those two are friends. I sometimes had to get on Heather's case because she'd be following him around the store when she should have been setting up an end-unit. Even after she got married, she'd be off in a corner talking to him."

"She's married? Where's her husband?"

"I haven't been able to make contact. The only phone number that I have for her is her cell phone, and she left that here in the store. We figured his number would be programmed into her phone, but the key pad is password protected."

"Thanks, Mr. Wozniak, can I talk with the officer again?" The assistant manager handed the phone back to the uniform.

"What's going on, Darnell? It doesn't look like there's been an abduction, and no one's filing a missing person report. It looks like it might just be an HR problem for the drug store. It's just odd and they're being careful."

"Normally I'd agree," said Wilson, "but there's an open case, a murder, that has a tie to someone who's been in employee areas of that store. Do you remember three years ago, a Lakewood woman was found dead in the truck of her car at Edgewater?"

"I was just new to the force, but I remember that."

"We figure that started as an abduction in the Fourth Ward. It's happened three times, always on the same date, the tenth of September."

"That's tomorrow."

"That's why I'm pushing every button I can. This woman doesn't fit the profile for the victims, but Wakeman asked me to see if there were other pieces lying around."

"What do you mean *victims*? I only remember one."

"That was the third. All older than this one, same date, three years apart."

"Oh, and this is year three."

"Exactly. So we have no missing person report, a nondescript light colored van, and an employee who may be playing hooky. It may just be an ordinary sort of weirdness, but I don't want to live with the guilt of not being paranoid at the right time."

"Got'cha. I'll try to track down the husband and the name of the floor guy, but I'll probably fall asleep on the job tomorrow."

"In other words, I'm going to owe you."

"And, I won't let you forget it!"

"I'll tell you what. If something comes of this, I'll put you up for cop of the year. If nothing comes of it, I'll remind you that your reward is in heaven!"

"How 'bout a good word to Wakeman?"

"Sure, I'll be glad to speak to Boyd," Wilson smiled at the use of his supervisor's first name. He remembered its affect when Megan used it.

"Boyd!"

She got it, thought Darnell.

Chapter 32

Six

All he wanted was a shave and a twenty minute power nap. *Is that too much to ask?* Darnell wondered as he reached for the buzzing phone that lay on the nightstand near his head.

"Detective Wilson?" said the voice on the other end. "This is Kevin Wozniak from Wallace' Pharmacy. You spoke with me last night."

In an instant Darnell was alert. Up until this point he was unsure if Mr. Wozniak had a first name, but he was more interested in what information would command a six o'clock phone call. "Yes, Mr. Wozniak, I remember."

"I'm sorry to call so early. I waited until six, but maybe it's important. Anyway, I woke up in the middle of the night and it struck me that Richard, you know the guy with the van that I thought I saw on the video, I remembered that when he cleaned the floors he sometimes wore surgical shoe coverings. I don't know why I didn't think of that before. I was going to wait until a decent hour to call, but my wife said that it must be important if you came to the store to ask about it."

At least your wife is smart, Wilson thought. "You did the right thing," he said without uttering the expletive that would have come more naturally.

"Well, I figured that four o'clock was just too early, even if you did give me a card with your number on it."

At four o'clock the call would have been more useful. That was about the time that he met Heather's husband on the front sidewalk in front of their apartment. The guy kept turning his face away when he spoke. Darnell guessed that he feared a DUI more than the news that his wife was missing.

"Mr. Wozniak, this is important. Can you find out Richard's last name?"

"I got that," said Wozniak in a voice that didn't sound early morning. "*Kosten*! That's his last name. I called the pharmacist at one of the twenty-four hour stores. He used to work my store and started working extra shifts at night once his kids got to college."

I don't really give a damn how you got it! thought Wilson. *I just wished you'd remembered two weeks ago!* "This helps a lot," was what he said instead. "He's mid-twenties, right?"

"That's right. I'd say about five-ten, dark hair..."

"That's fine; you've been very helpful I'll get back to you if I need any more info."

"I'll be at the store at two," said Wozniak.

Now is not the time to get chatty, thought Wilson. "Thanks, I'll remember that" and he ended the call. How many twenty-something Richard Kostens with light colored vans could there be in Cuyahoga County? When he hung up from the call to the dispatcher, he knew he would have a plate number and an address in a few minutes. It might take a little longer for a warrant to search a residence, but waking a judge was a part of the risk of his job. His next call, however, was to Megan. She insisted on being informed, and had only a little more sleep than Darnell.

"We have a name!" he began.

* * * *

Davis was more of a morning person than Beth. He was aware of her sacrifice as he tried not to pace. He was trying to guess what he was about to face at the hospital. The cliché of *pulling the plug* on life support was not really descriptive of good medical care. As a result, he could not tolerate the TV shows that always had blood squirting and medical staff with the emotional maturity of seventh graders. People who live with death around them learn how to use humor as a form of emotional first aid, but they do not last in the profession if they have not come to some sort of arrangement with the reaper.

As a pastor he knew of people in his own profession who buried grieving families under heaps of words like *victory*, *power*, and *unending life* as though they could erase the reality of death. He suspected that their use of the words of faith to avoid the significance of loss put them in the same category as the TV doctors and nurses. McGowan never confused the experience of faith with the mantras of the silly who used perfectly good words to avoid what they themselves would one day have to face.

He always understood that, most of the time, removal of life support was a critical period in the care of the family. If done too soon or too matter-of-factly, it fueled the second-guessing game of *maybe if we waited a little longer*. The best caregivers move at a speed to give dignity to the dying and assurance to the living. Davis saw his own role in this intersection of death and the world of the living. After holding on for dear life, there invariably comes a time to let go. Knowing *that* time is always more an art than science in spite of all the beeps and waving lines on the machines.

"I'll be ready to leave by six," Beth said, a little irritated by Davis' unconscious pacing.

"That's fine," he answered trying not to hear her annoyance. "I'm just thinking about what to expect. The Todds may think that this is going to happen like unplugging a computer and everything just crashes. I've never seen it work that way. If his heart is strong, he could go for hours, maybe days."

"But you said that he was pretty much brain-dead."

"He is, but the body has an impulse to life. The heart will try to keep everything going until every system shuts down. I'm sure they will keep him comfortable, but…"

"It may not go fast."

"No, and then the family wants it to be over, and then they feel guilty about *wanting* it to be over. I think this family has enough guilt anyway."

"Well, I'll be listening to Burt."

"I doubt it. He's pretty much out of it for an hour or so after he takes his meds. If the timing is right, he'll be back to his rare form when the Physical Therapist arrives so you can both try to keep him under control."

"You like him, don't you?"

"He's got a lot of bluster, but I suspect that I haven't really gotten half of his real story. Maybe the morphine will loosen him up and he'll tell you. What I can't figure out is how he and Helen ended up in Lakewood."

By six they were making their way toward Route 2 and the more or less straight shot into Cleveland. The road to the hospital, however, would be circuitous with stops in Lakewood and Public Square before meeting up with the Todds whose family crisis preempted the scheduled events of a busy day.

* * * *

Kosten knew that he was enjoying this too much. He should have been thinking of Rachael in these last hours, but Heather was such an interesting distraction as she lay sprawled on an old mattress he kept on the floor in his private room.

He had not known exactly what to expect with the effects of the medication. He thought that she might just lose all consciousness, but in her on-the-edge-of awareness state, he could get her to raise her arms as he peeled her tee-shirt over her head and raise her hips as he extracted her from those tight jeans. She only had the one tattoo, the tramp stamp that he had admired at the store when she bent over for his amusement.

She was on the pudgy-side, but it made her breasts fuller, and he liked the soft heaviness he felt when he squeezed and lifted the pliant flesh beneath her cotton bra. He could feel her nipples harden against his palms, and knew that she was getting aroused.

"No, Heather," he chided, "you'll have to wait until I get back." He liked thinking that in her stupor she was anxious for his attention, and he liked the idea of her being here when he walked back from Edgewater.

He sat with her all night and poured another drug-laced beer down her throat at 5:00 a.m. Finally, in an effort to clear his mind, he stood over her and masturbated. "Did you like that?" he asked as he wiped her off with toilet paper. She mumbled syllables of an unconscious language which pleased him. "Don't worry, I won't force myself on you," he said, "I know that you want it as much as me."

He did worry, however, that she might awaken while he was with Rachael, and maybe panic if the drug wore off sooner than he anticipated. He considered tying her down, but that would put her in the wrong mood at his return. He did not want her bruised when he pulled away the last of her wrappings.

In the end, he left her in her underwear. He would take her clothes with him, but left a handwritten note:

> *Heather, I am so sorry. I had no idea that the beer would get to you so quickly. I am sorry you got sick. I've taken your clothes to wash them out and will be right back. I figured that you would not want to go home with that smell on you.*
>
> *your Dickybird*

He was going to stick his finger down her throat so that she would taste the vomit in her mouth, but he thought better of it. He wanted the medicine to stay in her stomach, and did not want to risk the involuntary act of biting. He went to the kitchen and brought back a glass and a partially filled carton of OJ. He crushed his last tablet of alprazolam, and poured it into the carton. He also added a postscript to the note.

> *Drink some more orange juice to get that taste out of your mouth!*
> *-back soon!*

He thought that last part a nice touch, and kissed her before gathering up her clothes into a plastic grocery bag and heading out the door. He keyed shut the deadbolt to his room and re-hung the van Gogh print that concealed the lock cylinder. The door itself was a full-length panel that disappeared into the wood grain of the back wall. It was a little after six when he turned the key to the ignition. Coffee and a donut would help him center his mind to the work of the day. After all, this was his mother's special birthday.

Chapter 33

Seven

"Richard Kosten, residence at 206D Arbor Avenue, econ-series, white van, license number SDVP-2904," Boyd Wakeman announced the information to the assembled group. As he was speaking, word was going out to the active patrols. In an earlier time it would have gone out as GPI, General Police Information, in the form of a radio code, but since 911 and Katrina, the codes were being abandoned in favor of plain language in an effort to bridge the differences in code dialect between jurisdictions. This announcement went to laptops mounted in patrol cars and text messages for the neighborhood police on bikes.

The urgency that Wakeman and Wilson felt was not actually underscored in the language of the message. They wanted to find Richard Kosten, but he had no conviction record and no outstanding charges filed against him. He *might* be the ghost image on a camera in a "case" where no missing person report had been filed. He was but a *person of interest*; a man who wore shoe coverings in a drug store. Haunted by the memory of a serial killer, Wakeman would word his request for a warrant in terms of extremely vague certainty, and with the hope that the Judge would be in a charitable mood.

In the meantime, Agent Sorento was playing hooky and Detective Wilson was off duty. Both were casually parked in front of a yellow-bricked apartment on Arbor Avenue. There were no white vans on the street or in the back alley.

"And now we wait," said Darnell.

"Are we already too late?" asked Megan. Neither one wanted to answer.

* * * *

This part of the game was always the most invigorating. Attending to detail gave Richard the edge. He liked outsmarting his Rachaels even if they were unsuspecting. He inventoried the few props he needed. The plastic zip tie was already coiled in his right side pocket. Latex gloves and surgical booties were folded flatly into his hip pocket making the bulge of a wallet. His left side pocket held exactly $1.19 in change, the cost of the coffee he would buy at the gas station. When he slid behind the wheel of Rachael's car, there would be nothing to slide out of his pockets to be left behind. The coffee would be swallowed, the money spent. The receipt for the coffee would be in the trash container next to the register. The shoe coverings and gloves would be on, and the zip tie would adorn the neck of his mother.

He touched himself at the thought that Heather was, even now, waiting at his apartment, but he shook that off with renewed focus on the adventure ahead. His cold shower was the equipment in the back of the van. He had removed the floor polisher which took up far too much space. In its place was a pressurized air cylinder to re-inflate the tire that he would flatten for his performance. This time, he also had a plastic bag for Heather's smock with its shiny Wallace Pharmacy name badge as well as her tee-shirt and jeans. He had folded them carefully as if they had just come out of a dryer at the Laundromat.

Rachael would leave her house at 7:41 to be at the bus stop by 7:48. The bus would then arrive in three minutes. Over the years, Richard had seen the bus driver actually wait as Rachael walked the final steps to the corner. She never *just* missed the bus. If she did not get on, it was because she did not intend to do so. Today, it would be different.

* * * *

"Burt, here is your medication. Beth's going to be sitting with you, so don't be surprised when I'm not here when you wake up," said Colleen as she put a white tablet in Zacharias' palm. He popped it into his mouth and sucked water through a plastic bendy straw to wash it down.

"Does she know the rules?" he asked. Beth looked from Burt to Colleen. She was already nervous at being a primary caregiver for a man she barely knew, even if it was only for a few hours.

"Prepare to have your leg pulled," Colleen said as an aside.

"Normally I am required to have an agent of the CIA present when major narcotics are being administered," said Zacharias with an absolutely straight face.

"Are they afraid you'll give away state secrets?" said Davis.

"They're hoping."

"Hoping?"

"Yep, they've been waiting for me to spill my guts about the inner workings of the KGB."

Davis realized that he was missing something. It was obviously a running gag, but one he was not in on. "Face it, Burt, you are a whole lot less interesting since the Berlin Wall came down."

"More's the pity," said Zacharias, "I miss the attention."

"Like you're not getting any now," she said.

"You lost me," said McGowan.

"Guess, he's not a fellow traveler," he said as if McGowan wasn't standing right there.

"He's playing one of his games," explained McQuisten. "We don't have time now, Burt. Davis has to get over to the hospital and I have to be the gofer for the Presbytery."

"Sounds like a normal day to me!"

"But you get Beth's company, so you'd better treat her well." Turning to Beth, she said, "He's all bluster. Besides, in a few minutes he'll be in gaga land. The therapist will be here in a couple of hours, so you'll get some relief if he's still feisty when he wakes up." She gave a glare at Zacharias that ended with a smile of practiced good humor.

"Don't worry about her," said Burt. "She'll understand my ribbing. She's married to him." He pointed to Davis. The four laughed at the truth of the statement.

"I don't think he'll be a bit of trouble," said Beth.

"I've left the car keys on the kitchen table along with the remote opener. If for some reason, you need to make a run to the store, you can. Call me at the church and I can give you directions. I've also left a list of phone numbers by the keys."

"Davis keeps telling me that you are super-organized. We'll be fine."

"Thanks, Hon," said Davis giving her a quick kiss. "I'll call from the hospital."

"What no kiss for me?" asked Burt.

"Sorry, Old Man, you're not my type!"

"I meant from her," he said pointing to Beth.

"Burton Zacharias!" scolded Colleen, who then leaned over and kissed the old man on the forehead. "You behave!"

"See how she treats me?" he sighed.

"You are a lucky guy," noted Davis.

"Yes, I guess I am."

"Just don't hit on my wife any more or your luck will run out!"

"Now, Davis," said Beth, "are you jealous? He is kinda cute."

Zacharias turned to Colleen, "See, I told you she'd understand my humor. Why don't you and Davis run along?"

* * * *

The drive to the Public Square was over by the time that Colleen and Davis had gone through their checklists of duties. It was only 7:30 when McGowan dropped her at the side door, and he was glad to see Jenks at the glass entry door to welcome her. With Colleen at the church, he had fewer worries about the church's schedule and could make the mental transition to the Todds who were probably already on the road toward University Circle. He headed east on Chester confident that he would be there ahead of them.

Chapter 34

All Ahead, Full

Richard didn't want to risk cutting the time too short, but he also didn't want his van on the street so long as to draw attention from the neighbors. He made his final preparations in the parking space closest to the privacy fence at the mom and pop store where he had purchased his coffee. Now the Styrofoam cup was empty, and he walked back toward the gas pumps where there was a trash bin right beneath the squeegee and paper towels.

He had backed his van into the space so that he would be unobserved when he walked behind the vehicle toward the rear passenger-side tire. As he passed the rear door, he took some pride in his technique for concealing his license plate. It was his own formula of lint and grit from the strainer of his floor scrubbing machine. The waste was easily peeled away from the screen filter like the pulp of homemade paper, and he carefully draped it over the end of the plate concealing the numeric portion of license. When dry, it conformed to the painted metal and held with the tenacity of dried egg yolk on a hot knife.

If ever stopped by a cop, it could be easily explained away by the buckets and rags in the cargo bay. His interest now, however, was the rear wheel. He bent down and unscrewed the black plastic cap on the valve stem. His pockets were mostly empty except for the oversized zip tie, so he uncoiled it and used its nylon tip to depress the brass pin. The hiss of the tire's exhale blew the rubber smell of stale air into his nostrils. He did not want the tire completely flat. He did not want to bend the wheel or cut the rubber. He simply wanted the visual effect of a driver in need, if not distress. He wanted to park what appeared to be a disabled vehicle in front of Rachael's door, and then be able to inflate it quickly from the compressed air cylinder van. The idea was to be on the street for as little time as possible.

These Rachaels were all alike. Alike when they agreed to help a nice young man in need. Alike when they took him back to where their cars were parked, and alike when he rolled their bulk over the metal sills of their car's trunks. After that there was little to do but slam the lid, walk back to the curb, inflate the tire, drive around the block to park the van. He always changed his clothes in the van before walking back to the Rachael car. He didn't want to appear to be the same person if someone had been watching from a neighbor's house. He would always allow fifteen or twenty minutes to pass before walking up the street, with a key in his pocket, a key that would take the two of them to Edgewater Park.

This would be his fourth such trip, and he thought about sitting on a bench for awhile and looking at the lake. There was an exhilaration that came from the idea of sitting nearby with Rachael resting quietly in the trunk. In any case, there really wasn't much reason to hurry. The car wouldn't be discovered until the park closed at dark. What was the hurry? Heather was *the hurry*. She might wake up and read his note. Her breasts were very soft and full, but he mustn't think about that now.

He drove slowly west on Detroit and then north on to Severn where Rachael lived. The van could have handled a higher speed, but if someone were watching, the limping gait would be more authentic for a blowout on Detroit that would be remedied here.

Richard pulled up on the apron of Rachael's driveway, jumped out of the van, and stared with disgust at the rear tire that bulged like a flattened bladder against the pavement. He swung open the rear door to the cargo area, and withdrew a long face that was turned toward the house. He started toward the front door. It was 7:45 and Rachael would be dressed for work, ready to walk toward the bus. He wore a blue scrub suit on top, blue jeans and sneakers below. From his neck on a bright red lanyard was a laminated photo ID with his picture and a logo from Cuyahoga General. It was, of course, counterfeit, and, although it would gain access here, would not get him down the corridors of the hospital. He pressed the doorbell that he knew to be in working order. A woman answered the door.

"You're here early," she said looking at the dangling ID.

"I'm sorry," he began. This was not Rachael and why was she expecting him? "My van has a flat tire," he said.

"Oh," she said, "I thought that you might be the physical therapist."

This was not Rachael.

His stunned look made her start again. "You are *not* the physical therapist."

"No, no," he said. "I'm on my way to work at the hospital and had a flat tire. Sorry, but it looked like someone was up here and I thought I'd ask if you had a lug wrench." His confidence returned with his voice. "I have a spare, but I don't seem to have a lug wrench to put it on with."

"Well, I don't know if..."

"Please," he said, "my boss will kill me if I'm late. If you have a car, you'll have a lug wrench in with the spare tire."

"I..."

"Please," he insisted. "I can get it myself if you show me your car. I'll use it here and give it right back not like my pranky friends who set me up," he added for veracity. This was not Rachael, but it was September 10th and she looked like a Rachael.

Beth remembered the keys on the kitchen table. "Walk around the side of the house," she said pointing toward the driveway. "I'll open the garage door and meet you out back." She closed the door and walked back toward the kitchen. As she passed through the dining room she spoke to Burt, "I'm just running out to the garage. I'll be right back." Zacharias murmured, but she had the feeling it was to a conversation somewhere in the recesses of his memory. "Sweet dreams," she said as hurried through the open doorway to the kitchen where she pushed the button on the remote transmitter. Through the open windows, she could hear the hum of an electric motor and the groan of the lifting garage door.

Kosten walked toward the drive that ran along the north side of the house. He heard the garage door before he saw it. He reached into his pocket and withdrew the coil. *This will work*, he thought.

Chapter 35

University Circle Hospital

Davis had been wrong on his timing. He was at the hospital at his intended time; he was just wrong about the Todds' arrival. Ruth had not been able to sleep and grew increasingly agitated at the prospect of Abe's dying before she made it to the hospital. The only assurance that Dan and Ben could give was to drive her to the hospital at four in the morning. The hospital staff was accommodating. The explanations for an early arrival that the boys had prepared went unvoiced; the ICU staff seemed to be expecting them. They understood.

At one point the chaplain on duty came to visit. She sat with the trio and stood with them when they passed through the doors that stood between the waiting area and the glass walled room where Abie lay resting peacefully in spite of the hissing and clicking that came from both the ventilator and the inflatable mattress that relieved pressure points and potential bed sores.

The chaplain spoke with the medical personnel. They explained that there was no reason why they couldn't go ahead and begin the process of disconnecting life support. Already, the family was aware that there were fewer tubes. Abie looked more human and less like some sort of junction box for the interface of machines.

"We'll wait for Rev. McGowan," Ruth explained, "I want to ask him something, before we do anything," she added.

The chaplain didn't push the matter. She was glad that the Todds had support from their local church. When Davis arrived, he remembered to turn off his cell phone before making his way down the now familiar corridors. He was surprised to see the Todds had already arrived and that they were not alone. The uncertainty on his face did not go unnoticed.

"You must be Rev. McGowan," said the woman whose nametag read Sandra Reston. "I'm one of the chaplains here at University. Ruth, Ben, and Dan have been visiting with Abe, but I'm sure they'd want to see him again with you before we remove the ventilator."

He couldn't acknowledge it aloud at the moment, but he was impressed by Chaplain Reston. In one sentence she had acknowledged the family by name and told him that the final crisis had not yet come. "Thank you," he said.

"I'll leave you now," she said. "If you need anything go to any phone and dial 2278, and it will come through on my cell."

"Thank you," said Ruth Todd who stepped up to take Davis' arm. "Rev. McGowan, I talked to Jack Dawson at the funeral home. He asked me who was going to perform the service and I didn't know. Ben and Dan thought maybe you would be willing."

The remark was worded as a statement, but McGowan understood that it was a question. "If that's what you want, I'd be proud to do it," he said.

"That's what I want," she said. "I know that you didn't know Abe, but you've been here at the last and that means a lot. I guess we should tell the nurse that we are ready."

Two of the ICU staff emerged from the unit. McGowan recognized one from the day before. They explained again that their intention was to remove all life support. That Ruth had signed off on this, and did she or the family now have any second thoughts?

"No," said Ruth. "This is Rev. McGowan," she offered. The attendant nodded. "He's going to perform the funeral."

It did not strike Davis as odd that Ruth's thoughts were already beyond a death that had not yet happened. He saw this a lot with people in these situations and supposed that it gave them a sense of direction beyond the mental disconnect that came with the decision to let go of life. In an hour or so, Ruth would be a widow perhaps paralyzed by the prospects of her future. To have a plan in place is a hedge against the unknown.

Davis was wrong about the *hour or so*. As they entered the unit, the supervisor saddled up next to him and said, "He's going fast."

McGowan was glad to see the boys on either side of their mother as she stepped toward her husband's still body. The machines had been pushed to the side. McGowan caught a glimpse of the plastic bag that hung beneath the bed frame. He still had a catheter, but the reddish tinge of the urine told him that he was still bleeding internally. A battery case the size of a cigarette pack was tucked neatly in the breast pocket of his gown and extended spaghetti-thin wires to the monitoring leads beneath the fabric. A red glow on his index finger made Davis look at the monitors for a number with a percent sign. *Seventy-eight* was the number. Even with the pale green cannula under his nose, he was not getting much oxygen. The only other attachment was the ubiquitous *R2D2* stationed beside the bed to infuse IV solutions and medications.

McGowan thought Abe looked much better. Yesterday, he was naked and full of drains. Now he seemed quiet.

"I thought they were going to take all this off," said Ruth who was unused to a hospital environment.

"They have," said Davis. "These are just monitoring devices, and the IV is so that they can give him something if he seems to have any pain." He didn't, however, seem to be in pain. If he was experiencing oxygen deprivation, it did not show in restlessness or hallucination. He was quiet; his breathing shallow.

Davis offered a prayer. He was pleased when, one after the other, they all told the dying man that they loved him. "I'm sorry," Ben added. Davis patted him on the shoulder.

A sustained tone brought back the tech who silenced the alarm. The nurse took out a stethoscope, listened, and nodded to McGowan. "Bless you, Abe," she said as she deftly removed the last of the tubes and wires. It was over.

"You may stay as long as you wish," said the attending physician. "We have your instructions to contact the funeral home, and that will be done. As you know, we will first have to conduct an autopsy, but that will not take long. Your husband had extensive injuries. It's a testimony to the emergency personnel that he made it this far."

Ruth nodded. Davis caught a reflection off her cheek. "We'll see you then," she said to Davis.

"I will visit and we can talk about the service," he said.

"It may not be until Monday or Tuesday," she said.

"That's fine," he answered, "I'll talk to the people at Dawson Funeral Home." With that, they were gone and McGowan had to twist around his emotions and mindset. He was supposed to be at a conference on spirituality. That was several miles away, and he figured that city traffic could be his excuse for making his way back slowly.

Chapter 36

Captain Hugh Mulzac

All Ahead, Stop! was the order and the seaman next to Burton Zacharias let out a string profanities that ended with a question: "What in hell is the Captain thinking?" he asked. "We're sitting ducks out here."

The night sky was blazing and the flames silhouetted a Liberty Ship. Burt thought it was the *Mulzac* on fire, but that couldn't be right. Mulzac was the Captain, not that burning torch, everything got so turned around.

"Doesn't matter," Zacharias barked back, "He's the one doing the thinking and he's the Captain." He could feel the hot wind coming across the water. There were men in the water. He could see it like an old movie. A Tin Can was screaming at a target in the distance and the U-boat would be busy for awhile. In the meantime, these poor bastards would sink one by one if the *Booker T.* kept up its sixteen knot crawl.

"Zacharias, get those cargo nets over the rail." The disembodied voice of the Captain was giving orders. He used his rigging knife to cut a piece of line in order to lash the heavy rope netting to the rail. He tried to lift the bulk of the hemp strands over the side, but something was blocking him. The hot flowing air was pushing against him.

"Give them something to grab hold," said the Captain, but still he could not push. He quickly looked about the deck and saw a heavy sheave. With one hand on the rail he reached out and just managed to get the outstretched fingers of his right hand under the edge of the bale on the pulley. With all his might, he pulled it around, pivoting it on the fulcrum of his shoulder. It crashed over the rail and dropped down, down over the freeboard until it hit the water below.

"Grab hold, you sons of bitches," he shouted with a fury. He lifted his leg to go over the rail and climb down the cargo net and pull up anyone too weak to grab, but his leg collapsed under him and he fell hard against the deck.

"Burt!" Came a cry from below. It was not the Captain this time; it was a woman's voice, or maybe an angel's.

Chapter 37

9-1-1

Davis thought about trying to track down the chaplain, Sandra Reston, to thank her once again. He always thought that people so far removed from congregations must feel very isolated from the people the serve. They see them once or twice, often, as in this case, to be turned away by other relationships of longer duration. The ironic thing was that she knew the Todds nearly as long as he had, but now he would have to prepare a funeral meditation to memorialize a stranger. She was probably with another patient already, and he was past due down at Old First.

Had he stopped to talk with her, he would have been there to get an urgent message from Colleen. A 9-1-1 call had been placed from Burt's house and the police and EMTs had been dispatched. She had tried his cell phone, but that went directly to voice mail.

When he reached the parking garage, he turned the phone on and it immediately started beeping. What he had intended as a leisurely ride down the Euclid Corridor now turned into race to meet all the signals on the run without triggering any traffic cameras.

The church phone was answered by a voice he did not recognize and the man said that Colleen had already been driven back to Lakewood by the Presbytery Executive. That meant one fewer stop, and explained why, as he approached the house, he saw Colleen getting into the side door of an ambulance. The EMT drivers were adjusting their paraphernalia around a cloaked body on a low-riding aluminum gurney.

"Davis!" McGowan turned to see Beth running toward him.

"Something happened, I only left for a minute and Burt got out of bed, he took a terrible fall." She threw her arms around her husband and choked the rest of her words into a string of indecipherable sounds. Davis just held her tight.

As they stood there, a couple in a black car pulled into the place along the curb where the ambulance had been. The man was African-American, well-dressed, and carrying a determined look as he moved straight toward Beth and McGowan. The woman with him got out on the passenger's side and began leisurely strolling through the trail of wrappers left by the squad and along the side of the house.

"I am Lakewood Detective Darnell Wilson," he said as he withdrew his laminated ID photo. "Can you tell me what just happened here?"

Davis looked at Beth. "I just got here myself," he said. "I'm Davis McGowan, this is my wife, Beth; she was here when it happened. Apparently Burt Zacharias took a bad fall. He just had hip surgery."

"I'm looking for information about a white van," said Wilson. "It crashed into a parked car at the north end of the street. The neighbors up there called 9-1-1 about the same time as someone called from here. It's very important. The man driving the van is a person of interest and I need to know if the two events are connected."

At these last words, Beth's composure returned. "There was a young man who came to the door," she said. "He had a flat tire. I think it was a white van."

"Darnell, look at this," the young woman called across the lot. Wilson began to move in her direction; the McGowans followed.

"This is Agent Sorento of the FBI," said Wilson.

The invocation of the three initials gave Davis pause. "What's going on here?" he asked.

Before an answer could be given, Megan pointed to the ground. An ivory colored zip tie lay on the ground like a long, narrow crescent blade.

"It was in his hand when I turned around," said Beth. "I turned when I heard Burt calling from the window."

"What happened after that?" asked Sorento.

"I was heading toward the garage," continued Beth. "He had a flat tire and needed some kind of wrench off the jack of the car. Burt's car was out here and I figured he wouldn't mind. All of a sudden there was a huge crash and Burt was at the window yelling something like 'son of a bitch' and I turned, and the young man was running back to his truck. He probably dropped that on the way. Anyway, he took off flat tire and all; Burt must have really scared him."

Megan and Darnell exchanged knowing glances. "I need to get a statement from you," Wilson said. "Pretty much what you've just said. Can you tell me what the man looked like?"

"Young, dark hair, good-looking. He had a hospital ID that he showed me."

"Write down as much as you remember. This is very helpful."

"But what about Mr. Zacharias?"

Any answer that Darnell might have given was cut off by the ring of his cell phone. He turned and walked away leaving Megan with the McGowans while he spoke to whomever was on the other end of the conversation.

"We know that you'll want to get to the hospital to see your friend," said Sorento, "what you're doing now is very important, and, in time, we'll be able to explain it better to you. Can you show me where you were when you turned around?"

"Sure," said Beth. "I was back toward the garage." She pointed up the driveway and instinctively began walking back toward the garage.

Along the edge of the concrete, just beneath the shade of the arborvitae hedge, Megan saw something shiny, and stopped the procession. "What's this?" she asked.

Davis started to dive toward the metallic glint. "Don't touch it," Sorento warned.

This must be serious, thought McGowan, who stepped back like he had just uncovered a coiled snake.

Megan got down on all fours to look beneath the branches without touching.

"It looks like it's polished brass," she said.

"It's a bell," said Davis. "It's engraved with *S.S. Booker T. Washington*. It was on a table next to Burt's bed. Up there." He pointed up at the first story window which opened on the room where a hospital bed stood in the place of the dining room table. "He must have thrown it out. There was a screen in that window."

"It's here," said Megan. It was lodged between two bushes about four feet off the ground. "He must have hit that pretty hard. How old is he?"

"Eighty-seven," said Davis, "He's told me that more than once."

"He has an arm on him. I wonder what he saw here that made him do it."

"He was pretty much out of it," said Beth. "He had taken his pain medication and was pretty groggy. He's recovering from a hip replacement. I was supposed to be watching him, but I left to get some kind of wrench out of the trunk of his car for the young guy with the flat. After I heard the crash, the guy behind me was running down the drive."

"Did you see him drop this?" asked Megan as she pointed toward the nylon zip tie.

"I don't know," said Beth. "All I could see was Burt looking like he was trying to climb out the window. That's when I yelled and ran back into the house."

"Would you feel comfortable putting this in a written statement, or would you rather make a digital recording?"

"I can write it out," said Beth.

"Good, I'll get a form and I'll sit with you while you write. Let's get away from here, though. The police will want to cordon this off until all these objects are documented."

Davis was about to ask whether this was a bit over-zealous for an old man knocking out a screen when Darnell returned from his private phone call. He was carrying a clipboard with blank forms for a witness report.

"We got him," said Wilson to Sorento. McGowan's sudden epiphany must have shown on his face. *This wasn't about Burton Zacharias; this was about the stranger in a van.*

"If you would help your wife fill these out," Darnell said, handing the board to Davis who took it without comment and turned to Beth.

"Where was he?" asked Megan in a more urgent tone.

"When he left the scene, he must have walked straight back to his apartment. He probably figured he'd have some time before we traced the vehicle and he could report it stolen. Didn't expect that we already were watching the place."

"What about the warrant?"

"I expect that will come very quickly now that the cashier's clothes were found in the back of the van.

Wakeman has pulled a few more people in to scour the area between the wreck and the apartment. Hopefully, they'll turn up a few things."

"Latex gloves and booties."

"Exactly." Darnell's phone rang again. "Is she there?" he asked. "They got inside," he said as an aside to Sorento. Then added, "She's not there."

"Why would he keep her clothes? He's been so careful about details."

"A memento?" said Wilson.

"Maybe," said Sorento, "but if he's keeping trophies you can bet he has some from his previous kills. He probably has a concealed stash. Have them check for panels in the back of the closets or drawers."

"No closet in what seems to be his bedroom," said Darnell.

"No closet at all? Is the room small? Is there a false wall?"

Darnell relayed Megan's stream of questions, and it was not long before a smile crossed his face. "Bingo!" he said giving her a thumbs up. "He didn't want them to break the door. He's given them the key. She's there! She's alive!"

Sorento and Wilson let out a simultaneous hoot and high-fived each other. It looked more like a response to a long-awaited Browns' touchdown than the decorous conduct of proper law enforcement. Every head turned in their direction.

"Sorry," said Wilson, "I just saved $300 on my auto insurance." Everyone understood that part of the joke and laughed for the wrong reason. Megan and Darnell just stared into each other's faces and reflected all-knowing grins. Only Davis wasn't taken in by the ruse.

"What's really going on here?" he asked, stepping up to the two private celebrants.

"We can't really say right now, sir," said Darnell. "It'll probably come out in the paper before we'll be able to say anything on our own. I'll just say this: your wife has witnessed something and it sounds like she has been a good observer. Just be aware that there are parts of this that she hasn't completely understood. When that hits her, well, she may need some strong support."

"Why? What did we miss?"

"Once she finishes her report, go see your friend, the older gentleman. Let's just say that he saved your wife's life today."

Chapter 38

Police Escort

Beth, Colleen, and Davis spent most of the day at the hospital with a very rowdy Burt Zacharias whose main complaint was that he had just jumped this hospital ship and why in the world did he ever get shanghaied back. Obviously, he remembered nothing, but his new hip was already in need of warranty repair.

Colleen called the boys to let them know what had happened, and they both immediately took leave from their jobs and flew into Cleveland.

Davis, for his part, did not turn off his cell phone and answered the call from the Dawson Funeral Home on the third ring. The funeral for Abraham Todd was scheduled for Monday morning at 11:30. Jack Dawson was anxious to know if Davis was planning to drive his own car or ride in the hearse. McGowan wondered why the question was such a priority. Most of the time where he was in the procession was a detail that could wait until the day of. Dawson's next comment solved the riddle. "We already have forty-two squad cars in the honor guard."

"That's quite a tribute," said Davis.

"Mansfield, Toledo, Bowling Green, they're coming from all over. I imagine that it'll be a solid line of cars all the way from the Funeral Home to the cemetery on Bogart."

"I'll ride with you in the hearse, then," offered McGowan. "That sounds the least complicated." While he was still thinking about it, he called Ruth Todd to set up a time when the family would be together to talk about the service. He would meet them at their home late Saturday morning.

It was nearly 4:30 when they left Burt and drove Colleen back to the house. The neighbor who had agreed to lock up after the police left, didn't have much to say, and everything was back in place except for a shattered bell, a window screen, and the wayward zip tie which had garnered so much attention. The police activity was of less concern than Zacharias' condition.

"He's scheduled for surgery on Friday," said Colleen. "That's tomorrow," she added as if no longer certain about the linear progression of time.

"Yes," said Davis.

"I wonder if everything went okay at the church," said McQuisten.

"I think we can let that one go," said McGowan, "get some rest."

* * * *

On Friday, the morning paper reported two unrelated squad runs. One was an elderly man taken to the hospital after a fall. The second, a traffic mishap that ended in the pursuit and arrest of a suspect in a missing person investigation. The cause of the accident was an under-inflated tire that blew out when the driver hit a curb and popped the seal that held the bead to the rim. The missing person was found drugged, but in good condition. Her name was being withheld until all the details were known. The driven of the van was a Richard Kosten, age 27 of Arbor Avenue. Nothing else was reported.

Davis doubted that this was the end of the matter, but was relieved that no one was calling the hospital to get the *elderly man's* take on the story. Maybe they already knew that all they'd get from him was the *real* story of the *Booker T.* More important was the fact that they were not asking Beth for any of the details about how her life was saved by a quirky turn of events. Davis was not really sure about the details of that part of the tale. And he was willing to remain ignorant if it would protect Beth from the realities that he first imagined when he had heard the words *he saved your wife's life today.*

There comes a point, for some people, when they are able to step outside themselves and into a more defined role. Actors make transitions as they apply makeup and costumes in order to assume a new persona. In the moment of the drama, that persona is more real to them than the bundle of clothes in the dressing room. Spock and Data amused Trekkies with their assertion of absolute logic in the face of emotion. In reality, this is not a science fiction. Plato wrote of Socrates' application of logic in the face of death, and caregivers play their own brand of Russian roulette by emptying a chamber of emotion to survive another day.

McGowan remembered the feeling. He had forty-two police cruisers being arranged for a procession, several hundred parishioners waiting to be moved by the eloquence of his Sunday sermon, and an old man who nearly climbed out of a window to save his wife's life. In each case, he was to be the calm voice of reason. Calm was not the problem; at times, reason was.

On Saturday he met with the Todds. He did not doubt their familial affection nor the fact that Abie's death had, in some ways, brought back a son. He went to the funeral home to meet Jack Dawson. Their conversation evolved through the professional expectation to the human. At the end they were laughing together like friends rather than professionals. Dawson confessed that he really hated Abie, a cop who bullied adolescents for fun. "He liked coming up on parked cars and shining his flashlight in our faces," he said. "It was even worse when I was younger. He would always hang out at Carl's Barber Shop. I remember sitting in the chair and Abie comes in and says, 'You can tell when they've been masturbating by the way their hair grows, right?' At that point, Carl starts fluffing my hair and says, 'This one's been really bad! Be careful, son it causes blindness!' Everybody in the shop laughed. I went home and started combing my hair different every day."

"Welcome to life in a small town," said Davis. "Every kindness and every cruelty gets magnified by the fact that everybody knows everybody."

Dawson took some comfort in those words. "I guess so, but when you've grown up in a small town…"

"The whole world gets small," offered McGowan. "It was sport; it was teasing, but I know that's not how it felt."

"No," Dawson said, "I lived in fear all through high school, and for what?"

"I've lived in small towns and I've lived in metropolitan areas. When I was in small towns, I wanted to get to a big city where I could be anonymous. Life is easier when you are nobody. I've really surprised myself by retiring to a small town. For all the gossip, nobody cares about me. I can have all the advantages of a small town with all the anonymity of a big city."

"But you are somebody! You are big time in Cleveland!"

"You can't believe small town rumors," laughed McGowan. "I'm your neighbor, Jack, that's all."

* * * *

That evening, Davis and Beth dropped back into their familiar pattern of driving out to Sawmill Creek Resort for the live band and dancing. September in Huron is still boating season and the band was relying heavily on classic Buffett. The other couples who practiced the same ritual were there, but the McGowans made a few apologies and sat on the upper level of the dining room and away from the dance floor.

There might be questions about the "cop killer" and what did Davis know? Beth was blaming herself for leaving Zacharias' bedside. "From what you said," Davis offered, "he was pretty persistent. Even if you were right there, you might not have been able to stop him from falling out of bed."

"But he threw that bell; how heavy do you think that was?"

"Not that heavy, a pound or two. He was reacting to something and that's what we don't know."

"He doesn't even remember exactly," said Beth, "he just says he saw his old shipmates and that was worth the hip and the bell." They maneuvered around the subject of Richard Kosten. At some level they were both conscious of the fact that the seemingly benign young man was arrested for abduction of a young woman, but they were clever enough to invent plausible excuses.

"Apparently, they knew each other or worked together," said Davis. "Maybe it was a boyfriend-girlfriend, jilted lover thing."

"I think it's probably something like that," agreed Beth, "Can't think he'd be interested in me, I'm old enough to be his mother."

"Hmm, that doesn't put me off. Wanna dance with an old man?"

"Sure!" she said, "but the only one I know just had his hip worked on."

"Guess you'll have to settle for me, then." He offered her his hand as the moved toward the dance floor. Everything was just too raw at the moment, better to surrender logic to trusted affection.

Chapter 39

Work Week

Nine-to-five people constitute an endangered species in an age of twenty-four hour shopping and electronically embedded office equipment. Still, in the minds of some, the week begins on Monday and Sunday is the last of the old week's hurrah.

Over the generations the *family blue-laws* had relaxed in Davis' case, but he took little benefit from it. The Holiness Codes of the Bible prohibited *work* on the Sabbath, but that was Saturday. In her Christian rendition, his Scottish grandmother would not allow her children to play noisily on Sundays. His father had cut back the prohibitions to no playing *guns or cards* on Sunday when it was his turn to parent. As a member of the clergy, Davis' experienced only a blend of the worst. There was little time for play on Sundays unless you counted chaperoning youth groups as entertainment, and there was certainly no prohibition of work. Today he would preach two services, make a quick circuit of the hospitals to see the most critically ill, make notes for a funeral meditation, and be in Huron for visiting hours at the Dawson Funeral Home. Any complaints on his part always sounded unspiritual, but only a sadist would call it a day of rest. It was work that needed to be done. The perception of the laity never quite fit the reality of the minister. They would come to church for rest, inspiration, and social interaction. The pastor could stand in the same room and be on show and at everyone else's beck and call. In the distant past he remembered trying to keep up with the Browns in a January playoff game while driving between nursing homes where he was serving communion to elderly shut-ins. He had videotaped that game, but never watched it when the Cardiac Kids skipped a beat at the end. It was not that he disliked the elderly, and he would certainly do it again if it meant a playoff berth for Cleveland.

Beth had elected not to go to services at Old First. She did not want to face the questions. Then again, the prospect of being alone all day was equally distressing. She called McQuisten who had gone to Saturday evening Mass at St. Lukes so that she could visit Burt in the hospital. She was anxious for Beth's companionship to break up the monotony that set in during Zacharias' dozing, so she was at the hospital when Davis was sitting in his office and trying to visualize an honor guard of active duty police.

He went back to a topic prayer book that he had from the seventies. It had special prayers for all groups and classes of people. There were prayers for professionals of all types, prostitutes, those suffering *sexual confusion*, and addicts. The closest career to law enforcement, however, was for people in the civil service. Why had he not noticed this at the time? It struck him how easily people, even prayer writers, could be blinded by cultural whim.

Abie Todd may have rattled adolescents, but he was not a *pig*, and he certainly did not deserve to die such a needless death. McGowan was grateful to the police who came to Zacharias' house, and, if the paper was correct, saved the life of one, maybe two women. He did not know what he could do to help Beth. At some point, another layer would be peeled back on the events of the past days, and his job was to be a husband, not a confessor.

On the drive back to Huron, Beth told of her visit with Burt, Colleen, and as it turned out, Bobby, Hugh, and the detective from Lakewood.

By the time Davis arrived, the only other visitors were the two boys and Colleen. The atmosphere was electric and Burt was his old self again. The McGowans needed to get on the road, however, and had to make a quick exit to arrive at the funeral home when the family would be there alone.

"The boys are really fun," said Beth. "They really made Burt rally. They are more like brothers than upstairs/downstairs neighbors."

"Why was the detective there?" asked Davis.

"He wanted to talk to Burt. Dr. Shafer pronounced him fit for questioning, but I'm not sure how much help he was."

"What do you mean?"

"Only that Burt says he doesn't remember anything except a very vivid dream. He was back on his ship, as he said. They were in a convoy and one of the cargo boats was hit with a torpedo. The destroyers went after the sub, and the Captain ordered their ship to stop to pick up survivors. It sounded perfectly normal to me, but Burt kept saying 'That's really weird isn't it?' I finally had to ask why he thought that was so weird. He said that convoys couldn't stop. The ships that were hit were just left to sink or drift. The rest had to keep moving. 'That's what was so weird about the dream,' he said, 'I was going to finally be able to do something.'"

"And that's why he was at the window? He thought he was in the middle of some man-overboard drill?" asked Davis. "That's odd."

"The cop didn't think so."

"What do you mean?" Davis could sense Beth fidgeting in the seat next to him.

"I don't want to scare you," she said carefully after a long pause, "but the story in the paper about the girl being abducted—well, that's only the part they know for sure. So, they've arrested him for *that*, but they found other things in the place where he took her—newspaper clippings and car keys—I don't know how it will all fit together, but there will be other charges filed. The detective thinks he'll be put away for the rest of his life. So, he's not going to come and get me or anything..."

"Get *you*? What do you mean?"

"Just don't freak when I tell you that they suspect that this guy has murdered women before, women my age. He stalks them."

"Well how could he have been stalking you?" There was a long silence.

"Not me, Colleen. I was just a last minute stand-in."

"And Burt saw it."

"That's what Detective Wilson thinks. Even in his haze, Burt realized that something was happening and incorporated it into his dream."

"What did the Old Man say to that?"

"He was plain insufferable. He was so happy about 'pulling somebody out of the water' that he went on and on."

"It was you he pulled out."

"And Colleen, she would have been the one if any of the craziness of the last week were rearranged."

"I guess I should write a thank-you to the Presbytery for that workshop. It's turned out to be the best thing I never attended."

"We've seen him before."

"Who?"

"Detective Wilson. He was with that FBI agent when we went to dinner at the Blue Point Grille. We were trying to figure out if they were a couple. Turns out they were trying to save our lives."

"Did you tell him that?"

"No, but I'm sure he's the man. Gives me a whole new perspective on that night, and on cops."

"And tomorrow, I get to bury one."

Chapter 40

Unexpected Ending

The procession from the funeral home to the cemetery was a major exercise in logistics. The service itself was not crowded, but when the flag-draped coffin was wheeled down the concrete ramp to the waiting hearse, Davis led it through a gauntlet of uniforms. Retired or not, Abraham Todd died in the line of duty, and no one was willing to split hairs over whether or not he should even have been on the scene when an out-of-control adolescent struck him blindly.

The sky was open and blue over the lake with a thin band of white drawing a crayon mark to measure the shoreline. At final count, there were forty-eight police cars ahead of the funeral coach. Their blue strobe lights reflected off the sunglasses of the citizens who lined the parade route. That's what it seemed to McGowan. This parade, however, was ominous in its silence. No sirens sounded and no onlookers cheered. As they drove past the barber shop, Davis wondered what Jack Dawson was thinking. He was seated next to him behind the wheel.

"They do support each other," Dawson said as if on cue. McGowan took him to mean the number of departments who sent representatives.

"It's overwhelming. I can't help but think that it will provide some sense of comfort to Ruth and the family."

"She's a sweetie," said Dawson.

They must have arranged a temporary detour on Bogart Road, because as they approached the cemetery entrance, the advanced party of squad cars split right and left to line the sides of the country road. The funeral procession approached the gates driving down the center of the road. The officers stood at attention on the traffic side of their vehicles until the last car had passed through the gates into the burial grounds.

At that point, the cars from the other districts flowed away along the tributaries of the highway system and back to their own jurisdictions. The Huron Police and Fire divisions were the pallbearers and honor guard at the grave site, and they fired the salute, collecting the brass casings and tucking them into the folded flag that the Mayor presented to Ruth on behalf of a grateful country.

At the end, Davis stood by the casket with the family. Jack Dawson quietly told them that they could stay as long as the liked, but they had had nearly enough. They pulled roses from the spray atop the steel casket. Dan and Ben helped Ruth back to the limousine. When the car started away, Dawson reached in his pocket for his cell phone.

"This thing has been ringing since we got here," he said. "Fortunately it's on silent mode. Only the office has this number and it better be important." He played with the buttons until a message came up. "It's a text," he said, "and it's for you. You are to call Colleen as soon as possible. The number is here."

"I know the number," answered Davis. He was reaching for his cell phone that had been turned off for the last several hours. He stepped away from the casket and out from under the canopy set up by the vault company. He selected McQuisten's number from the list and hit enter. She answered on the second ring.

"Colleen," he said. She spoke before he could phrase his thoughts.

"Burt is dead," she said. "I knew you had a funeral, so I called Beth and she gave me the number."

"What happened?"

"The boys and I were there. We'd had a good visit, and Burt insisted that we go down to the cafeteria and get something to eat. We'd been gone less than fifteen minutes when someone came looking for us. They think he threw a clot that went straight to his heart. It happened so fast."

"Where are you now?"

"We're still at the hospital, but I think we'll head back to the house. There's nothing we can do here."

"Would you like me to come to the house?"

"I can't ask you to do that," she said. "You are busy enough."

"You don't have to ask me," he answered, "I'm offering. I know it would mean a lot to Beth. She's pretty wrapped up in this, too."

"Yes, thank you. I'd appreciate both your being here." Davis ended the call.

"Jack, I was invited back to Ruth's house for a light lunch. I don't know if you were planning to be there..."

"I'll tell them that there was a death in your congregation," Dawson said.

"Thank you."

"Some days are like this in both our businesses," he said.

"Too many," answered McGowan.

* * * *

"Dad left us his *sail plan*, as he called it," said Hugh. He placed a small steel lock-box on the dining room table which now dominated the living room of his Lakewood double. He turned a key and lifted the hinged lid.

"He gave me a key to this when my mother died, and told me what I'd find inside. Every time I came home, he'd make a joke of asking to see if the key was on my ring. 'A place for everything,' he'd say, and ..."

"Everything in its place," interjected Davis. "Of course, if everything isn't properly stowed, how would you find it? He was a man of the sea, wasn't he?"

"Shipshape and Bristol fashion," agreed Hugh, "and this box proves it. He has all his powers of attorney, a living will, his bank account numbers, funeral instructions, car titles, and house deed. Over the years I've gone over everything with him, and he always swore me to secrecy."

"Secrecy?" said McGowan, "he never seemed to have a problem speaking his mind to anyone who'd ask."

"For normal stuff, but never for anything he thought was really nobody's business but his own."

Colleen had been quietly sitting and not getting into the lightheartedness that Hugh was trying to invoke. "That's because of what happened after the war," she said. Having spoken, she had to elaborate.

"He was a merchant marine. According to him, they were trained to a higher standard than the navy, but they weren't military, they were private citizens. Hugh and Bobby have heard this before, many times."

"They had higher casualty rates than all the branches of service combined," said Bobby, "but they were *a brotherhood, a union of men*, he'd say and they were paid civilian wages. At the end of the war they were granted none of the benefits for education or jobs that the other vets got."

"He went back to the west coast," said Colleen, "stayed in his trade. Then the *Red Scare* came along and he was branded *Communist*."

"What?" said Beth.

"Their union was blacklisted. *That's* when he came to Cleveland. He couldn't stomach the accusations after what he had seen in the war. He came here to be near water, but away from the coasts. Met Helen here, she really brought him through his anger at the government and authority. After that he became an advocate for the lost people, that's why he took in Jerry and me, put up with all that craziness." Her voice trailed off.

"And you returned the favor," said Hugh. "Dad had his own version of crazy. Anyway, since Davis is here, I think you need to hear his instructions for the funeral. It's to be the same as Mom's. At the church, if it's possible. He said any of the ministers at Old Church would do, but he'd prefer one who was *not too religious and no assholes*–those were *his* words, not mine. I think he approved of you, McGowan."

"Thanks, I think," said Davis.

"Dad was a seaman," Hugh reminded, "If you couldn't tolerate a little rough language, you probably weren't worth the effort.

"And, this is important. He wanted the bell struck twenty-two times."

"The bell!" said Davis. "It was taken as evidence, and who knows what shape it's in. I'll get a bell from the marina store, but it won't say *Booker T. Washington*."

"Any port in a storm," said Hugh. "Why am I falling back on Dad's clichés?"

"Because it is the duty of the crew to follow orders," said Bobby. "See, I can do it too. He's here and he's given you the *sail plan*, didn't you say? And the proper response is..."

"Aye, aye," they all called in union.

The tasks were easily divided. Colleen called to reserve the church. Davis called the funeral home that Burt had indicated. He found that the service had been prepaid at the time of Helen's death, and that the director had the same copy of service plans that Hugh had given, but without the verbal exceptions with regard to clergy. McGowan also called the Lakewood police to see if a bell could get released from the evidence locker, but that was not possible given the current interest in events of the previous week.

Counting the land lines and cellulars, the five had seven phones between them. They called all the numbers in an old handwritten address book that Burt kept in the drawer next to his bed. Most of the names were by a woman's hand; many were crossed out. Hugh called the three uncrossed names with the not-so-cryptic initials *BTW* in the margin. They were the last shipmates of a proud ship. Each of them asked who would be ringing the bell.

The service was set for Thursday morning at 11:00 with an hour for visitation prior to the service. It was nearly 8:00 in the evening when Bobby offered to call out for pizza, and no one could think of a single argument against it.

"Do you have this week's sermon title, Dr. McGowan?" said Colleen. The two laughed at the fact that the routine requirements would move ahead on them whether they were ready or not.

"Not yet," answered Davis. "But my secretary won't need it until Tuesday."

Hugh Mulzac Zacharias came out of the kitchen with a tray loaded with several shapes of glasses, a liter of cola, a bottle of Merlot, and a thirty-seven year old single-malt whisky. "We've worked hard," he said, "but I'd like to do one thing more. Honor my father with a toast."

Everyone stood unasked. Hugh poured out the scotch. It was, after all, Burt's favorite. He raised his glass. "To my father, Burton Zacharias of the *Booker T. Washington*," he said.

"Here, here."

"To the lives he saved," said Bobby, "including those in this room." His eyes went to his mother, Colleen who returned the glance and tipped her glass. Davis looked to Beth.

Davis spoke next. "I am going to use a word that nowadays is used too easily and is rarely understood, but your father embodied its true meaning." He raised his glass, "He was *a man*."

They all sat in the silence that follows a blessing, but the postlude called them to attention with the sound of the doorbell and pizza. Davis raced Bobby to the door to grab the check. In the ensuing clamor, Colleen leaned over to Hugh.

"I know you'll want to get the estate settled," she said. "Just so you know, I've made plans to share an apartment with an old girlfriend," she said. "You will be able to put the house on the market whenever you want."

"I don't think that'll be legally possible," said Hugh. "Dad left the house to you."

"He can't do that!"

Hugh laughed. "Too late to stop him now! He did that eight years ago. Swore me to secrecy, said he'd have no peace if you knew because you'd be always trying to talk him out of it."

"But that's not fair to you."

"Dad was right, you'd have been unbearable. I'm afraid it's just plain out of my hands. Not only do I agree with his decision, I signed off on it with the lawyer when he wrote it up. My only concern is that you let me visit."

Colleen hugged him like a son. "This is always your home," she said. She hurried out to the kitchen as the others returned with the pizza. She came back when she had regained composure. She carried a liter bottle of soda to cover her retreat. "Thought we'd want this to drink," she said to the twisted woosh of the plastic cap.

Chapter Last

Epilogue

Thursday morning Davis was in his office, but Colleen was not at her usual position as gatekeeper. She was getting ready to process into the sanctuary with the family of Burton Zacharias. On Wednesday, Bobby's and Hugh's wives and children had arrived in town, and spent hours going through family photos and remembering more pleasant times.

The reception desk was in the charge of Donna Adams, the church educator who had stepped forward to take the pressure off Colleen. McGowan could hear Donna's voice in the outer office.

"Dr. McGowan is preparing for this morning's funeral service."

"Yes, I know. That's why I would like to see him. We have something he may need." Davis recognized the voice. It was Detective Wilson, who had spent so much time trying to piece together the events of a week earlier. He got up from his desk and walked around to the door. Agent Sorento was with him.

"Dr. McGowan," said Darnell. "We have this on loan, but we'd appreciate your not telling anyone that we brought it to you." In his hand he held a small cardboard box. Davis could guess the contents.

"Come in," he said. "Donna, these are the investigators who took care of us when… Burt fell, I guess you could say. Detective Wilson and Agent Sorento, am I right?"

"Perfect," said Sorento, "but since we are not officially here, we're *Darnell* and *Megan*." Darnell walked into McGowan's office and burst into laughter. Facing him on the desk were three brass bells bearing the engraved name of a ship, *S.S. Booker T. Washington.*

"Looks like we got here too late, Batman," said Darnell to Megan.

"They surprised us, too," admitted Davis. "They represent the last three survivors of the crew. We called them to tell of Burt's passing and they all asked about the bell. I told them that it had shattered in a fall. I couldn't see telling them that he had actually used it to break out a screen. Without our asking they each overnight expressed them to the church. They came yesterday."

"Well, you're right about the shattering," said Darnell as he opened the box. "The pieces are big and fit together okay, but I don't think it will chime."

"If it's alright with you, I'd like to set it in line with the others during the service. It still has a lot of meaning."

"That's fine. We will be in the audience, though, and will have to take it back after the service."

"This seems over-and-above on your part. Could I write a note of commendation to your supervisors?" Megan and Darnell exchanged knowing glances.

"Let's just *say* they already know and would prefer not to have a paper trail," said Sorento.

Darnell hesitated, and then asked: "What did he die of? He seemed pretty robust when I saw him."

"It was a blood clot, something that just broke free and went to his heart."

"Why didn't they code him?"

"He had a Do Not Resuscitate Order. He had said his goodbyes and sent his family off to get some lunch. And he went. Somehow it seems to fit with a man who always refused to live life on someone else's terms. He cared a lot less about himself than in saving others."

"He did save others," said Wilson softly. The three stood in the silence of that moment.

"You know," said Davis changing the subject. "The other day Beth pointed out that we had seen you two together before. We were eating dinner at the Blue Point, and you were seated near us." The two exchanged looks, and McGowan knew that he had outed them. "Anyway, we were playing that old married couple game. We were trying to decide whether you were on a date or whether you were working together on some project."

"What did you decide?" asked Megan.

"Well, it went back and forth. I thought the discussion was too animated for a date, so I thought it was business. Beth thought you looked pretty interested in each other. That's sorta how we left it."

Megan took Darnell's hand. "You were both right."

About Cleveland

When I was growing up in North Olmsted, Ghoulardi was warning us about knifs, and the brick office building on Brookpark Road, just east of the Valley bore the initials NACA rather than NASA. During the course of my first career, I lived in New Jersey, Pennsylvania, and Southwest Ohio. When my writing career started to take off, however, I came back north. The family ties are no longer here, but it's the place where I choose to live. Davis McGowan, the protagonist of three of my books came along for the ride. In a sense, his experience of the north coast mirrors mine.

It's always safer for a fiction writer to keep all the imaginary characters in imaginary places. There is a part of me, however, that thinks this story is about life in the Western Reserve. We are all aware of the Cleveland of the jokes, but maybe the joke is really on the naysayers. A few years ago, my wife and I had visitors from Menton, France. It was a fine summer day near the lake, and they made the remark that it was the *même chose Côte d'Azur* (same as the Riviera). In good self-deprecating fashion, I said, "come back in February." The truth is that I like the change of seasons and the moods of the lake, and I want the people who read this book to feel familiar with the place. As a result, I name some actual restaurants and landmarks. (What I say about them comes from their websites, so, if dinner sounds good, they are in the phone book, too!) On the other hand, the names of the hospitals are all wrong, and you will not be able to find the apartment building on Clifton where Richard Kosten used to live. This is fiction, the characters are not real, and the events did not take place. Many of the places, however, exist and those who really want to see a Greater Cleveland may see some of it more freshly through Davis McGowan's old eyes.

As ever, I owe a debt of gratitude to Nancy Brady my editor and writing critic, and to Chuck and Jackie Duffy who traipsed around the Westside and Public Square to make me more current on some of the detail. A tip of the hat goes to Ray Ritter, who keeps a boat in the slip next to mine, and suggested dinner at the Blue Point Grille. I should also thank the Reverend Bob Bates, a colleague serving Old Stone Church who was also one of my predecessors at First Presbyterian Church in Fairborn, Ohio. Finally, Jean-Luc et Denise Lo Cicéro who have followed McGowan through his adventures and insisted that he learn more about serial killers.

RBS

Rob Smith currently lives and writes on Ohio's north coast. He enjoys sailing, and when not working on his novels, he is refurbishing an 1850's house which was built by a ship's carpenter turned lighthouse keeper. In addition to his prose, he is also known for his poetry. In 2006 he won the Robert Frost Poetry Award from the Frost Foundation in Lawrence, MA. He holds his undergraduate degree from Westminster College in Pennsylvania and master and doctoral degrees from Princeton Theological Seminary.

Davis McGowan made his first appearance in *McGowan's Call* which was published in 2007.

To learn more about the author, visit his website at: SmithWrite.net

PHOTO CREDIT:
NANCY SMITH

LaVergne, TN USA
27 February 2011
218093LV00001B/2/P